WALTZING MATILDA

WILLOW ROSE

Cover design by Juan Villar Padron,
https://juanjjpadron.wixsite.com/juanpadron

Special thanks to my editor Janell Parque
http://janellparque.blogspot.com/

**To be the first to hear about new releases and
bargains—from Willow Rose—sign up below to be
on the VIP List.** (I promise not to share your email with
anyone else, and I won't clutter your inbox.)

- Sign up to be on the VIP LIST here :
http://bit.ly/VIP-subscribe

Tired of too many emails? Text the word:
"willowrose" to 31996 to sign up to Willow's VIP text List
to get a text alert with news about New Releases,
Giveaways, Bargains and Free books from Willow.

Chapter 1

JOHN ANDERSEN LIKED to say he was at the bottom of the food chain. A bottom-feeder. It was things like that they said about themselves, you know—plumber to plumber—while smoking behind the shop. They'd make jokes about it and say stuff like, *Your crap is my family's bread and butter;* or *Every time your toilet won't flush, you put food in my mouth;* or John's favorite, *Plumbing is the only profession where you can take a leak and fix it at the same time.*

Other than the jokes, there wasn't much to laugh about in his profession. John Andersen had stopped enjoying his work many years ago. To be honest, he was sick of it. They were busier than ever around the island since more and more people lately had problems with their pipes and plumbing. Sometimes, John wondered if it was an age thing, if the pipes laid underneath Fanoe Island were getting too old. It wasn't unusual for John to be busy this time of year since the cold was starting to set in and often people's pipes would freeze overnight and even crack. But this January had been a lot busier than what they were used to. A lot.

John rolled the minivan up in front of the old building that housed Fishy Pines and killed the engine. He let a long sigh hiss through his teeth and took off his seatbelt. It was his last job of the day and, hopefully, it was going to be a fast one.

Tina, his wife, was waiting back at the house. She had dinner ready. Pork chops and mashed potatoes, his favorite, and he had promised to be home before six o'clock today. He looked at his watch. Half an hour. It was all he had and all he was going to give this.

John got out and grabbed his toolbox. A woman came out from the building and approached him.

"Are you the plumber?"

John nodded indifferently and pointed at the van that said Plumber-John in big letters. Next to it, a sticker said:

THE MAN
THE MYTH
THE PLUMBER

"So glad you're here," the lady said. She was wearing a white coat over her knitted sweater and he guessed she was a nurse. She could also be a doctor, but she didn't look like one to John.

The place was known around town as *the nut-case house*. It was where you ended up if things didn't quite add up inside your head, as John's mom had put it when driving by back when he was still just a kid himself. John remembered how he, as a child, would picture the people in this place. How they would sit in their chairs and rip out the hair from their head, pull it all out, while laughing maniacally and pointing at you with their crooked fingers, telling you that *you are up next.*

A shiver ran down John's spine as he walked up toward the front door and followed the lady inside.

"I understand it was some issue with the pipes?" he asked as the fluorescent light engulfed him.

The woman nodded. "Yes. Especially at nighttime. It keeps our patients up and, between you and me, the last thing you want in a place like this is grumpy patients."

John chuckled. "I bet."

"Let me show you where it is," she said, and he followed her to the door that had WOMEN written on the front of it.

Back when John was younger, he had often fantasized about what was on the other side of a door with that sign and dreamt of going in there. Back when he was a teenager in high school—and he didn't know toilets would be all he would see day in and day out for the rest of his life—he and a friend had even spied on the girls through their window while they were in there chatting and putting on make-up. But the janitor had caught them one day, and that was the end of that. John had served detention every afternoon for a year after that stunt, whereas his friend Max had somehow talked his way out of punishment. John had never been able to talk his way out of anything in his life. Most of the time, opening his mouth meant getting himself into more trouble. He realized that at an early age. So, ever since his teenage years, he had kept it shut unless speaking was absolutely necessary. It had proved helpful in marriage and in his work.

"It's this one," the lady said and pointed at the middle stall. She opened the door and revealed an old pink toilet, a Gustavberg anno 1931.

"This one makes a lot of noise. Like a thumping. It goes on and on all night long with no end to it. On and on. And it is clogged. We can't use it."

John looked down into it, then back at the woman. "It looks fine." He flushed it and it worked perfectly.

"Yes, right now, of course, it works. It stops working at the same time as the noise starts."

"What noise? I can't seem to hear anything."

The woman looked at her watch a little annoyed.

"It usually starts here at six o'clock and goes on for the rest of the night. It's like a loud banging noise, sometimes scratching. To me, it sounds like an animal might be trapped down there or something. But that's just me, I guess. We can hear it all over the building once it starts. In every room. That's how we figured it had to be the pipes. A colleague of mine said it had to do with the fact that the temperature drops as the sun goes down."

John nodded. It amazed him how many people were amateur plumbers.

"I don't know. I'm not a plumber," she continued. "But I do know we need it fixed as soon as possible. It's such a commotion and very unsettling for the patients. If you'll just wait a few more minutes, you can hear it for yourself."

John looked at his watch and thought of the pork chops. He was going to have a cold dinner again. There was only one thing he loathed more than cleaning people's pipes and looking into their toilets—and that was eating cold food.

Chapter 2

"IT'S PROBABLY FROZEN PIPES," John said. "They might have cracked. It's been happening a lot lately."

He got down on one knee next to the toilet. His knee complained. It was getting harder and harder for him to do his job since it had started to act up. They had always told him it would one day. It happened to all plumbers, they said. Especially with the changing winds when it got colder, then he would be able to feel it. Back then, when he was younger, John had just thought it was old nonsense. He was stronger than most and it would never happen to him.

John winced in pain as he plunged into position. The lady was still hovering above his shoulder. He hated when clients did that...when they stayed to watch him. It was like they believed they had to be there in case he needed help or just to keep an eye on him. There was only one thing he hated more than that and that was when they left money out in plain sight, just to check if he would steal it.

"So, you believe that would cause it to make that sound?" the lady asked. "If they are cracked?"

He sighed. The pain shot through his knee and into his body. "That could be it, yes."

The woman shifted on her feet and looked at him. "I have to go check on a patient. Let me know if you need anything."

Finally.

He didn't turn to look at her as he said, "Will do."

The lady's high heels clacked across the tiles as she left and finally John could get started. He wasn't going to wait for the sound. He could already tell that the toilet tank had cracks in it. It was no wonder. It was very old and so were the rest of them in this restroom. They were probably going to have to replace all of them within the next six months.

John knew how it would go. One of them, probably the one he was looking at now, would crack first, then spill water down the side of the toilet and on the floor. About one hour later, the entire restroom and the hallways outside would be flooded. Since those things mostly happened at night, the patients would probably wake up and put their feet into the rising waters as they tried to get out of their beds. It was going to be a lot more disturbing to them than a thumping noise from the pipes.

It wouldn't be enough to just replace one of the toilets. If they didn't replace all of them, it would happen all over again a few weeks later, once the next in line cracked. John had seen it before and he usually recommended that people replace all their toilets since they were often from the same time period, but for the most part, people couldn't afford to replace all of them at once and so he would have to come back once it happened all over again. It was their loss, not his since he would make more money that way, but it amazed him how people always refused to listen and thought he was just out to get more money out

You'll come a-Waltzing Matilda with me.

Prologue
FANOE ISLAND 1982

of them. He would often ask those people if they owned a canoe before he left the house.

John looked at the cracks in the side of the tank, then wondered if that could be what made the noise at night. Probably not, he concluded. There had to be more. It wasn't the reason for the clogging either. There had to be something stuck in the drainage. Probably just old dirt and maybe tampons that the patients tried to flush. He would recommend that the lady have them cleaned as well as put in new toilets.

John rose to his feet, straining with the pain, then turned around to put his tool back in the box. This wasn't something he could fix in this short period of time. It was a bigger job. He'd probably have to come back with several of his guys and it was going to be costly.

Maybe I will be home in time for dinner after all.

John sighed. He hated restrooms like these. They reminded him of elementary school. Those years hadn't been good to him. John had been a bed-wetter and occasionally he peed himself in class as well. An overactive bladder, his doctor had told him. He would grow out of it. But he hadn't until he was fourteen and it earned him nicknames like *Pee Bucket* or *The Urinator* in school.

John shook his head when remembering the days he feared going to school. Just the smallest tickling sensation inside made him wince. Constantly fearing, *What if I don't make it in time?*

John's back was still turned to the toilet when he heard it. He turned to look over his shoulder, tool still in his hand. He took a step inside the stall and looked down in the bowl. The water in it was shaking, splashing up against the sides. John took another step closer and stared into the bowl, where the water was rising fast while the thumping grew louder.

"What in the…?"

Now, John had seen and heard many things in his profession as a plumber, but never this. Not this strange sound that grew louder and louder and made it feel like his head was about to explode.

The rising water suddenly stopped just when he was afraid it might spill over, and that was when it was rapidly sucked out of the bowl, faster than any toilet could ever flush. Suddenly, the bowl was completely dried out while the suction was still going.

John rubbed his chin, his hands shaking slightly. The sound was growing louder like something was approaching, something big. He was wondering what inside the pipes could make that sound. He had never seen or heard anything like it.

He leaned over the bowl to better look down. He felt the suction grow stronger and more forceful, just as the thumping did the same. What he saw in the bowl literally made him stop breathing.

Oh, dear Lord!

Now, John had never thought he would ever wet his pants again. He could have sworn he never would.

But for the first time in thirty years, he did.

Part I

JANUARY, PRESENT DAY

Chapter 3

IT WAS GETTING dark and cold, but Susan hardly noticed. She was lying on the beach, her boyfriend Caspar next to her. They were listening to Sam Smith on her phone, each of them wearing one of the earplugs.

"I love this song," she said and giggled.

"Me too," he said with a deep sigh.

In front of them stood a dragon. A big black fire-breathing dragon, panting and wheezing. It looked just like the one in the movie *How to Train Your Dragon.* It was kind of cute, Susan thought. She wanted to ride it but wasn't sure she could stand up.

"Are you still tripping?" Caspar asked.

She smiled, blissfully. "Uh-huh."

"Mine wore off," he said.

He sat up and the earbud fell out. Susan stared at Toothless in front of her. It was fading in and out like it was deciding whether to be real or not.

"You wanna do more?" he asked and showed her the bag of magic mushrooms.

She thought it over for a few seconds, her mind spinning out of control. She kind of wanted to since she didn't want Toothless to go away. But at the same time, she had to get home soon. It was getting late. She had school tomorrow. They both did.

Caspar ate some, then handed her the bag.

She smiled and took a few, then chewed them. She laughed as Toothless came back in its full shape, then lay back down to look at it as it lifted off the ground and hovered above her. Susan had always wanted a dragon of her own. Who wouldn't love that?

Caspar grabbed her hand in his and squeezed it. Susan sat up, fast. She was suddenly feeling nauseous.

"I think I took too much," she said.

"You're fine," Caspar said, laughing. "Just tell the whale."

Susan chuckled, but her stomach felt wrong. She rose to her feet. Everything was spinning forcefully and made her even dizzier. Caspar was deep into his trip and didn't even notice that Susan had left and walked up to the dunes, where she fell to her knees and threw up.

As the entire contents of her stomach ended up in the sand, Susan suddenly didn't feel so blissful anymore. Nor did she feel like staying on the beach. She was freezing and needed a warm bath and bed.

"Caspar?" she said.

"Uh-huh," he said from the beach.

"I…I think I need to go home."

"Okay. Don't forget the stroller or the grandmother on the way," he said, tripping.

It didn't even make her chuckle. Her stomach was hurting, and she felt so thirsty, she could drink the ocean if only it wasn't so salty.

"I'm going now," she yelled at him but received no answer.

She struggled across the thick dunes, feeling dizzy and nauseous. She fell to her knees a few times, got up, and wandered off, relieved that she didn't have a long way home.

When she reached the asphalt by the closed ice cream shop and heard the footsteps coming from behind her, she thought it was Caspar and turned to look.

But it wasn't him. It was something else. Something dark and sinister, something shadowy. Just being in its mere presence made her skin crawl.

"W-who's there?" she asked.

She tried to scream as the figure reached for her, but no sound escaped her mouth. Even if Caspar had heard her, he would have only assumed it was part of his mushroom-induced fantasy. A conjecture he was going to regret for the rest of his life.

Chapter 4

"I AM SORRY. There is nothing more we can do for him."

I stared at Mrs. Kimberly in front of me, my jaw completely dropped. "Excuse me? You're telling me you're expelling my son, and all you can say is you're sorry?"

The principal shrugged. We were sitting in her office—like so many times before when she had called me in to discuss Victor's future. Her kids—her annoyingly picture-perfect kids—were smiling from inside a frame on the shelf behind her. I often wondered why she had a need to turn her back on her kids every day, but in this instant, I realized that was what she did, wasn't it? She didn't care that my son was in the spectrum for autism and that he needed extra attention, extra help.

She leaned forward.

"Miss Frost…"

"Emma."

"Emma. Your son is twelve years old now. He should be able to behave himself. He should know that this behavior is unacceptable by now. Lord knows we've discussed this many times before."

"I've told you," I said annoyed, "he didn't bring the knife to school because he was planning on hurting anyone. He brought it because he is scared. He has this idea in his head...there are these monsters, if you wanna call them that, these...beings that are targeting him. That's what he believes. He wanted to make sure he was protected." I sighed deeply, knowing I was fighting against all odds.

"He can't bring a knife to school, Emma. No matter the reason. You know that and so does he."

"He didn't even take it out of his backpack," I said. "He's been bringing it for months."

"And now it was discovered, when it fell out during class. It spread panic all over the classroom."

"But you know my son, Kimberly. He's a sweet boy. He wouldn't harm a soul. Can't you give him at least one more chance?"

"How many last chances have I given him so far?"

"Six," I mumbled, looking down. "But you have to help me out here. I don't know what to do."

"There's always Fishy Pines."

"No," I said, determined. "My son is not mentally ill. He's not going to be institutionalized. He can live a normal life."

Kimberly sighed deeply. "Who are you kidding, Emma? You've said that for years. Still, the boy gets more and more closed up every year. He still throws fits. He screams in class if someone accidentally touches him and he yells things out if people make a mistake. He's a disturbance."

"A disturbance? Is that how you see my kid?"

"Yes, Emma. You know I love Victor, but he can't seem to function properly in class. Not even with help from the Special Ed class. He won't cooperate with anyone."

"He's scared," I said.

"He suffers from anxiety," Kimberly said. "He needs medical attention and you're not giving him that."

"He's not sick. He just has a very vivid imagination."

She sighed again. It annoyed me.

"He's never going to make it through high school," she said. "There's no way he can do that."

"Why not? He can already do all the math and don't get me started on his reading. He's better than any high school student in most subjects. Science too."

"But his grades are not good enough," she said.

"That's because he doesn't like being in school. He can't focus, and he refuses to take tests because he…"

"Because he refuses to take orders from anyone, I know. He lives in his own world and he needs help, Emma. He needs real help, the kind we can't give him here."

I was biting my lip, worrying how to convince her my son was still able to make it through school. But, deep down, I feared she was right. Things had gone from really bad to extremely worse over the past year since his therapist Ole Knudsen left the island, and Victor seemed further away from this world than he had ever been. He spends all his time in the yard with the trees and the rocks, speaking to them, doing whatever he does with them and refusing to participate in anything in school. Was I really kidding myself thinking I could give him a normal life?

"I am sorry," Kimberly said. "As I said, there is nothing more I can do. I have recommended to the county that he be transferred to Fishy Pines. They have a program there that Victor might like. They know how to deal with someone like him."

She handed me a pamphlet. I pulled it out of her hand —forcefully—with a loud grunt.

"Someone like him," I mumbled and got up.

My son is smarter than anyone here. You just can't see it because —God forbid anyone is a little different.

Victor was waiting for me outside the principal's office. He was talking to himself when I got out there and didn't look up at me. He kept his head bent down.

"Come on, buddy," I said. "We're going home."

"But we just got here?" he said, then mumbled something to an imaginary friend next to him.

"The school has expelled you, Victor," I said.

He didn't react. He kept staring at the bathroom door next to the row of chairs.

"You're hearing it again, aren't you?" I asked.

He nodded.

I cleared my throat. "Come on, buddy. We need to go. This school isn't good enough for *someone like you.* You deserve something much better."

Chapter 5

I WAS STILL MUMBLING under my breath when we got home. Victor immediately ran into the backyard and hung out with his trees. Meanwhile, I made myself some coffee, mixed together the dough for some bread, and kneaded it thoroughly while imagining it being Principal Kimberly's face before I put it in the oven. I ate chocolates from a box I had received at Christmas from my publishing house as a thank you for a great year, while staring at the bread in the oven, grumbling about how idiotic and amateurish those teachers and the entire system was. I looked at the card on the box from the publishing house, then wondered if I should write a book about it. It probably wouldn't sell very well, not like my other books that had become multi-million bestsellers all over the world. The publishing house probably wouldn't even publish it. I was just so angry with them for throwing my boy out that way. And now what? What was I supposed to do? There were no more schools on the island. I couldn't homeschool the boy; that was out of the question. I didn't have it in me. I couldn't let him run around out there all day in the snow, talking to the trees. He needed an education. His problem was that he didn't have a diagnosis; there was no box he would fit into. He was too smart and too normal for the mental institutions, and too abnormal for the school. Wasn't there anything for someone who was just in-between?

I groaned and sipped my coffee, then ate more chocolate, and then Sophia walked in the door.

"Hey there, anyone home?"

I smiled. She walked to the pot and poured herself a cup of coffee. Alma was right behind her, running into the living room where I knew she would grab all Victor's old Duplo Legos that he never played with.

"So, what did they say at the school?" Sophia asked as she blew on her cup and grabbed a piece of chocolate. She would never let me eat alone.

"They threw him out."

"Uh-oh. It finally happened, huh?"

"I know. They've threatened to do this for years, but somehow always ended up taking him back. I really thought we could avoid it."

"What did he do this time?"

"Brought a knife to school."

"That's bad, Emma. That's really bad."

I grabbed two more chocolates and ate them both at the same time. "I know," I said with a deep sigh. "I know."

"So, what are you going to do?"

I answered with another sigh and grabbed the last piece in the box.

"I'm guessing you don't know," she said.

"You guessed right."

"You never told me what happened to that guy who worked with him?" Sophia asked. "He did some excellent work, didn't he?"

I nodded, annoyed. "Ole Knudsen, yes. He was so

good I thought he would change everything for us. He did so much good for Victor. But he left last year. Got a better job in Copenhagen."

Sophia shrugged. "Maybe you should move back there. I mean, I would hate to see you leave, but if that's what's best for Victor?"

"Victor hated the city. Maya loved it but would kill me if I forced her to move again. She has all of her friends here now."

"But she's a senior in high school; she'll be graduating this summer, right? And will probably soon…"

"Don't say it out loud," I said and looked at the empty box of chocolate. I craved more now as I thought about Maya and the possibility of her leaving home. I knew she would one day, of course. It was the natural way of things, but I couldn't bear the thought of my little daughter growing up and moving away from home.

"I don't want to think about it," I said and sipped my coffee.

"But she might go to Copenhagen to study anyway," Sophia said, not letting it go. "Then you would be close to her."

"But I love it here," I said. "I love our little island. I love the tiny ferry you have to take to get here and I love the people, even though they are very strange and stubborn. I can't leave this house. I love it so much and now I have finally gotten it renovated so it's just perfect for me. I love living on the beach and I love having a yard with big trees that Victor can play with. I love having all this space and eight bedrooms, Sophia. Eight. I never had eight bedrooms before. And my parents just moved here. Should I just leave them? They moved here to be closer to me and to the kids. Plus, did I mention that Victor hates the big city? There are not enough trees there. It's no place for him."

"Okay, okay, I get it," Sophia said with a chuckle. "I'm glad you're not going anywhere."

"And there is Morten," I said. "He can't leave the island. He won't. He loves being a policeman here. The big city would kill him with all its hardcore crime."

I chortled thinking about Morten running after drug dealers and gang members. It definitely wasn't his thing. He was a typical small-town cop, who knew everyone and enjoyed the calmness of the island.

"How are you guys doing?"

"Pretty good," I said.

"Are you going to move in together anytime soon?"

"We've talked about it. A lot. But it's difficult with the kids, you know? Jytte hates me like the plague and there is no way Morten can get her to come live here with us."

"But she graduated already," Sophia said. "She'll be out of here soon."

"So far, she's still here living with her dad, but as soon as that changes, I think we'll be ready to take the leap."

Alma squealed from the living room and Sophia got up. She walked in there, then came back holding one of Alma's shoes in her hand. It was half eaten.

"Not again," I said, then yelled, "Kenneth!!"

"He was eating it with my daughter's foot still inside of it," Sophia said. "You've gotta get a better hold of that dog. He's just as bad as the first Kenneth you had. Maybe even worse."

I scratched my head when I spotted Kenneth in the living room, ripping my new cushion to pieces and growling.

"Kenneth II," I yelled and ran after him. The dog let go of the pillow and ran out the French door leading to the back porch that Victor had forgotten to close. It was freezing in the living room and a little snow had been blown inside and onto the carpet. I closed it while looking at Victor out there. He was wearing a full body suit to keep him warm and I was glad he was because he was kneeling in the snow in front of a big tree, looking like he was in a deep conversation with it. He closed his eyes and took in a few deep breaths, inhaling the freezing air. I wondered if he was meditating or something, then let it go and turned around. Right in front of me sat Brutus. The big pit-bull with those bright glowing eyes of his, staring at me intently like he always did. He was so quiet, I never knew where he would come from or that he had entered the room. He was Victor's dog, whereas Kenneth version II was Maya's after Kenneth version I was killed a few years ago.

"Gosh, Brutus, you scared me," I said and held my chest. "Were you here the whole time? Did you see what Kenneth did? And you did nothing, huh? Well, that makes you just as guilty in my book."

I heard the oven ding and rushed into the kitchen and pulled out my bread. It smelled heavenly and it was ready just in time for Maya to come home; we could all have it with our afternoon tea.

"I gotta get home," Sophia said. "The kids will be out of school in just ten minutes."

"Have fun," I said, trying to imagine the hell it had to be for her, being alone with six children, having to feed all of them when they came home, trying to get them to do their homework and not fight while picking up backpacks and dirty socks from the floor. I was happy it was just the three of us in my house. This suited me perfectly.

Chapter 6

THE REST of the day was quite uneventful. Maya came home and wouldn't eat any of my bread, as usual, since it was filled with carbs and she was *cutting down on carbs*, whereas Victor ate two pieces with jelly on them, then rushed back to his trees. I had a couple of pieces too, telling Maya the carbs caught up to me many years ago, while Maya ate some fruit before she went to her room to do her homework.

Meanwhile, I returned to the room I had made my office and stared at the blank page on my laptop for a few hours, hoping for inspiration to strike, but it didn't. It hadn't for a very long time. It had been more than two years since I had last written anything, and it was getting annoying. Usually, I would write about things I had experienced myself, like my latest book *Where the Wild Roses Grow*, which was about what had happened to Morten and me when we traveled to Ireland for a vacation. It was probably the worst vacation of my life, but the book had turned out to be really good and became an instant bestseller. It made me a ton of money and I was good for a long time. So, it wasn't because I necessarily needed to write anything, but I was beginning to fear that I never would again. The past two years had been quite uneventful in my life, which I guess was good, but still. I had hoped I could just make stuff up like other authors did, but that was a lot harder than I had expected it to be.

Morten had the evening shift at the police station, so I knew he wouldn't be over for dinner, and I made it easy on myself and heated up lasagna leftovers from the day before for all of us. Maya mostly ate salad, but she was in a good mood and talked about her friends and who was dating whom. It was fun to hear about, but it saddened me that it was all about her friends and not about herself. Maya had never had a boyfriend and it saddened me slightly since she was almost eighteen now and—as far as I knew—had never been kissed by a boy. It wasn't because she wasn't attractive. She was a very pretty girl, but she wasn't ready for it or at least hadn't been for a very long time. She had gone through some tough times, losing her memory some years ago and never fully regaining it. There were still gaps in it, especially from her childhood, but it was becoming less and less evident. I wondered if she was just getting better at hiding it or if it was actually improving. Still, she struggled with her self-confidence and was a little behind the other kids in maturity. Plus, she struggled in school to get her grades up, especially in math since there was so much of the basic stuff that she couldn't remember. Life as a teenager had been particularly rough on her and it made me sad. I wanted her to enjoy high school and have a great time with her friends and be a normal teenager, but it just wasn't happening.

I told Victor to go to bed at nine, even though he didn't exactly have to get up early in the morning since he didn't have school. He still needed his sleep. Victor could be absolutely impossible if he didn't get enough rest. And I was the one who had to deal with him all the next day and maybe even the rest of the week before we found out what was going to happen to him.

I decided I would call the county and ask them what to do with the boy the next day. The problem was that I knew what they were going to say. They had already told me the same thing last year when the school threatened to expel Victor. Fishy Pines. He wouldn't even have to live there like the really ill did, but just go to the school. But it wasn't what I wanted for him. I didn't want him to hang out with kids who had tried to commit suicide or who were psychotic or manic or paranoid. He wasn't sick. Victor wasn't sick, I kept telling them. He was just…different.

I fell into some stupid TV show and wasn't done until ten-thirty. I walked the dogs on the beach while wondering how I was going to convince the county that Victor needed to be in a normal school. I wanted them to understand that putting him in the same school as mentally ill kids was going to destroy him. Because he understood the difference.

It was freezing outside, and the wind bit my nose and cheeks. The sky was completely clear, and I could see so many stars it made me almost dizzy to think about all the solar systems out there, all those worlds that we knew nothing about.

Sometimes, I felt like Victor belonged out there. He didn't seem to belong here.

I walked up in the dunes when suddenly I couldn't see Kenneth II anymore. I called him, but he didn't return as he usually did. Brutus, on the other hand, walked right behind me like always, staring at me with those light blue eyes that lit up in the darkness.

"KENNETH!"

I had put a small bell on his collar because he often got lost, and this way I could hear him up in the dunes. I walked towards the sound, calling for him to come when I heard him growling like he had when splitting my cushion to pieces.

He had found something and was eating it. I could hear he was crunching it. It was very loud in the quiet night.

I sighed and hurried up. I had once found him with a dead seagull up in the dunes and he had eaten half of it and rolled himself in it before I got to him. I had to bathe him three times before the smell finally got out of his fur. I could still smell it sometimes when I thought about it.

"Kenneth! You better come back here...now. If you rolled in something again...I will..."

I used my phone as a flashlight when I approached the dog, who had definitely gotten ahold of something and was growling while trying to rip it. As I got closer, I could tell he had dug something out of the sand. The stench of rot filled my nostrils and made me nauseous.

"Kenneth, let go of that," I yelled and shooed the dog away. Kenneth ran off, growling at me for ruining his feast. Brutus stayed behind me while I shone the light from my phone at the dog's findings.

I am not lying or exaggerating when I tell you that my heart literally stopped. Because what I saw there in the sand, between the dunes, was that terrifying and sickening.

Chapter 7

SUSAN WOKE up tied to a bed. She couldn't move her arms or legs, and something was covering her mouth, so she couldn't speak or scream.

Where am I?

It looked like a hospital, at least some part of it. The monitors and the tubes and the bed seemed like something from a hospital, but the room surrounding her was definitely not. The ceilings were high, more than ten feet, she guessed. They were gorgeous, decorated between the wooden pillars with beautiful paintings, making it look almost like a church ceiling.

Susan managed to lift her head and look around. It was a big room with lots of wooden furniture. There were bookshelves all the way to the ceiling and more books than she had seen even in the library downtown.

What is this place?

There were beautiful antique vases, a grandfather clock, a golden Buddha figure, what looked like some African art stuff, and clocks and watches in a glass display. Not ordinary watches, but hundreds and hundreds of old watches, in all shapes and colors, some very old, others new.

Susan grumbled and tried to get free, but she was tightly strapped to the bed. The medical equipment next to her seemed very out of place compared to all the collectibles and beautiful antiques in the room.

Help me. Someone, please help me.

She tried to scream but not much sound came out except muffled groans behind the gag.

Was she still high? She had taken too many mushrooms and gotten sick, she remembered that much, but maybe this was the mushrooms' work? Maybe she was still in the dunes, still lying in the sand and imagining all this?

Susan closed her eyes and tried to wake herself up. She had never been this high before. Once, she had tried to get home from a party but been so high she ended up in a bush because she couldn't stand still and the world was constantly spinning around her. She had woken up in the bush a few hours later, not remembering how she got there or how long she had been there. Was this like that time? Was she simply dreaming all of this?

Susan opened her eyes, wondering if she could force her brain to get her back to the beach, but she was still in the bed, still tied down, and the fat baby angels on the ceiling were still staring back at her.

How did I get here? Why am I strapped down? Did I hurt someone? Did I hurt myself? What is this?

Susan tried to close her eyes once again, but when she returned to the same spot when opening them, she began to cry. She felt helpless.

I want to go home; please, someone, help me get back home.

She heard a sound coming from the door at the end of the room. Susan stopped trying to get loose and looked. The handle moved. First, it turned left, then right, then left again. Susan's heart was beating so fast, she wondered if it could jump out of her chest. She watched the door as it opened slowly and someone entered the room, a shadowy figure moving swiftly toward her. As he came closer, she could see that he was wearing a mask of some sort to cover his face. A big plastic mask. As he breathed through it, he sounded like Darth Vader. As he reached out his hand toward her, she noticed that the skin on it was peeling and scaling. It was falling off like dandruff, and some of it landed on her black shirt.

Chapter 8

"IT WAS KENNETH WHO FOUND HIM."

I was still shaking while talking to Morten. I had called him right away when I saw the fingers that my dog had chewed on.

"I think he dug him out of the dunes. Or at least some of him."

Morten shone his flashlight at the arm that seemed to still be attached to the body. He had called for his three colleagues to come and help dig out the body, and now they had the boy's head and torso uncovered. I felt so terrible when looking at the bite marks my dog had made on the fingers and the hand. Morten's two colleagues pulled the rest of the body out of the sand and we all looked at one another.

"What the…?" I asked.

Morten knelt next to it, then looked up at his colleague Allan. There was something in the way they looked at one another that made me uneasy.

"Is that…?"

Allan nodded with a sniffle. "I think so."

Morten approached me. "Maybe we should get you home."

He was trying to protect me, but it was too late. The body was in bad shape; it looked strangely old and wrinkled like it was almost deflated, but I could still see who it was. His name was Asgar and he went to school with Maya; they were in the same class. He was one of the few that Maya found joy in spending time with and who actually seemed to be a good friend to her, and I had hoped they might start dating one day.

"That's Asgar," I said. "Asgar Dragstedt. Am I right?"

"Emma. You need to get away from here…"

"Am I right?"

"We don't know yet. We think so. It looks like him. But, of course, we can't say anything until it is confirmed. The forensics team is on its way from Copenhagen. You shouldn't be here when they arrive. I've taken your statement and you need to get back to the kids, Emma."

I agreed to let him take me and the dogs home, then got into his police car, the dogs in the back, me in the front.

"I didn't even know he was missing," I said, still shocked as we drove down my street. All the houses on the beach were so quiet and dark, in complete oblivion. No one inside of them had any idea what they were going to wake up to. It was this type of thing that would completely shock a small peaceful island like ours.

Morten shook his head. "Me either."

"But the body has been there for quite some time, right? I mean, it looked old; it was hard to even recognize him."

"No one knows how long he has been there," he said, his voice heavy. I could tell this bothered him. He knew these kids very well and had a daughter only two years older.

"Not till we get the autopsy results. For now, I will have to ask you to be discreet about this find. Don't tell anyone. Especially not Maya since we don't want rumors to run amok. Asgar's family needs to be notified first and then we'll have to tell the school and the kids somehow."

I nodded, heavy at heart. "Of course. My lips are sealed."

He sighed, leaned over, and kissed me. "All right. Get some sleep. I'll check in on you tomorrow once this quiets down a little."

"You really think it will quiet down?"

"Probably not," he said with a sigh as I exited the car. "Knowing this island, it will probably get pretty heated up in the coming days and maybe even weeks."

Chapter 9

I HEARD him before I even opened the door. Morten had already left when it began. His screams were ear-piercing. I stormed inside and slammed the door behind me.

"Victor!"

I ran up the stairs and into his room, the two dogs right behind me. Maya was already in there, sitting by his bedside, trying to calm him down without touching him because she knew that would only make everything worse. Maya looked at me when I entered.

"Mom, please. I can't make him stop."

"Victor," I said again.

He was still screaming, holding both hands to his head like there was something inside of it that was making him scream. I knelt in front of him, careful not to touch him.

"Victor, honey, sweetie."

"Please, Mom. I hate it when he screams like this. Please, make him stop," Maya said, her face twisted in anguish.

"I'm trying, Maya, I'm trying." I took in a deep breath. "Victor, honey. You've got to stop screaming, please."

His hands and legs were shaking, almost rhythmically. He lifted his head and his eyes rolled back, and as they did, he stopped screaming. I turned my head and spotted Brutus. He had entered the room and was sitting in front of Victor, staring at him. Victor's entire body was shaking heavily, and gurgling sounds emerged from his throat, sounds that soon became something similar to a word.

"What's that, Victor? Are you trying to say something, sweetie? What are you saying?"

The shaking intensified. I worried he would choke on his own tongue or have trouble breathing, but I had been through this before with him and usually, it stopped on its own after a little while.

"Please, Vic," I said. "Please, just come back to us."

And that was when the gurgling became real words, or at least what sounded like real words. His eyes rolled back down and soon he stared at me while he spoke. He grabbed both my arms and held them tight, so tight he was hurting me.

"It's happening," he said, spitting as he spoke. "It's happening again."

I stared at him, perplexed. What on earth was the boy talking about? Did he know I had found a body? Was that what this was all about?

"What do you mean, Victor? What's happening?"

He was still staring at me, but I sensed he wasn't really looking at me, more like looking into somewhere else. It was like he could see something I couldn't. And he was staring right at it.

"Rats," he said.

"Rats?" I asked as I looked at Maya, then back at Victor. "What do you mean by rats?"

"RATS!" he yelled and covered his face. "Rats are

everywhere. Everywhere. Get them off me. Get them
OFF ME!"

Chapter 10

I MANAGED to get him to calm down. If it was me or just because he wore himself out, I will never know, but Victor fell back asleep. I kissed Maya goodnight and sat on her bed while we had a short chat about Victor. I told her he wasn't doing so well and that he was going to have to get some more help in the future since they had thrown him out of school. I hadn't told her earlier because the last thing I wanted was for her to be concerned. She did too much worrying already and I didn't want to add more to it.

"So, Victor doesn't go to school anymore?" she asked.

"That's right. I have to figure out what to do with him," I said.

I looked into her eyes, then wondered how she was going to take Asgar's death. I feared that it would totally break her and that was the last thing I wanted for her. I thought about the coming day and what it would be like when the principal told them all about it.

"Mom. You're shaking," she said.

"Yes. I'm sorry," I said. I tried hard, but couldn't hold back the tears. "I'm so sorry. I am so, so sorry."

She sat up in her bed. "Mom, you're crying. What's wrong? Is it Victor? I can help you more if you need me to."

I shook my head, crying full-blown.

"Mom, what's wrong? I'm sure you'll figure something out. You'll find a school for him."

"That's not it," I said and shook my head. I wiped tears off with my sleeve, then grabbed Maya's hand in mine.

"Then what is it, Mom? You're scaring me."

"Something happened. I promised Morten not to tell you, but I think I need to. I can't send you to school tomorrow knowing this…"

Her eyes grew wide. "What are you talking about, Mom? You're freaking me out. Tell me what it is."

I held her hand in mine, rubbed the top of it, then sniffled. "It's Asgar."

She wrinkled her forehead. "Asgar? What about him?"

"I know you've known him for years and you two have grown pretty close, so that's why…"

"Mom! Tell me what is going on. What happened to Asgar?"

I took in a deep breath. I knew Morten would be angry with me for this, but maybe he didn't have to know. Maya wasn't the type to run out and tell everyone anyway.

"Oh, sweetie…he's…he is…they found him. In the dunes. "

"Who found him?"

"Actually, it was me. Or it was Kenneth II. I heard him crunch something and then I walked up there and saw… him…or parts of him."

"Just tell me, Mom, what happened to Asgar?" Maya said, annoyed.

Our eyes met. "He's dead, honey. They found his body in the sand."

I could tell she didn't believe me. She kept staring at me, her eyes skeptical, then, as they softened, she said, "He's…dead?"

I nodded and held her hand tightly in mine.

"Oh, sweetie. I am so, so sorry…"

"But…he's skiing with his parents," she said.

"Skiing?" I said with a sniffle.

"Yeah, they left last week for the Alps, as they always do this time of year."

"No, sweetie. He isn't skiing…he's gone, Maya."

"No," she said. "He went skiing with his parents. I mean…he did, didn't he?"

"I don't think so."

"But…he was supposed to be with his parents? You're telling me they left without him?"

"Maybe," I said, sniffling. "I don't really know."

Tears sprang to Maya's eyes. "I can't believe he's gone. I can't believe it. You're sure it was him?"

I nodded. "I'm sure."

Chapter 11

HER MOTHER TOLD her she didn't have to go to school, that she could stay home today, but Maya wanted to be there. She wanted to be at the school when they told everyone.

It happened at one o'clock, after their lunch break. Maya spotted her mother's boyfriend, officer Morten Bred-balle, as he walked across the school courtyard and, shortly after, they were all told to gather in the gym.

"What do you think is going on?" Maya's friend Christina asked as she came up next to her. Christina was new in town and had only been at the school for a few months. Maya liked talking to her since she never had to worry about her asking her something or talking about something that happened when they were younger. It was just easier to hang with her than the others. Maya didn't like being reminded that she had suffered a memory loss. She wanted badly to move on.

Maya shrugged. She felt another tear escape her eye and wiped it away. She had been crying a lot all night and had a hard time holding it back in class, thinking about Asgar and glancing at his empty chair in the classroom.

He had been in love with her. He had recently told her so when they had met downtown for brunch at Café Mimosa. It was just two weeks ago, on a Sunday. It had been freezing, she remembered, and his nose had been so red it reminded her of Rudolph, and she had giggled at him when he said the words. He had taken it the wrong way and been hurt. She had grabbed his hand in hers and held it tight, then told him she didn't know if she loved him back, but that she liked him. A lot. But the fact was, she felt so confused and broken inside, she didn't even know if she was capable of loving someone. At least not yet.

It had ended badly. He had run away from her, out of the café, and even though she had texted him every day since then, he hadn't answered. Before his ski trip, he hadn't even looked at her in school. Losing him had made her feel lonely, but somehow, she had always believed they would be friends again at some point. That he would forgive her and they could go back to being best friends again.

"We have gathered you all here today to bring you some very sad and disturbing news," their principal opened.

Maya felt more tears approach and sniffled to hold them back. Christina looked at her, then back at the principal, who now told them that they had *lost one of their own*.

Maya felt the waves of shock as they rushed through the crowd, but she wasn't listening to the words anymore. She was crying full-blown as the alarmed faces around her turned to look at one another, the principal's words bouncing off the walls of the gym, magnifying them, making them almost screaming at Maya. Gasps and shocked grumbling went through the crowd, from one to another as the realization sunk in.

"I can't believe it," Christina said and clasped her mouth.

"Me either," Maya said, crying.

Her eyes locked with those of Samuel, Asgar's best friend, who was standing not far from her. He and Maya had shared a kiss once at a party three months ago. Maya had enjoyed it, but been filled with such deep guilt since they both knew Asgar was crazy about her. They hadn't spoken about it since and she had promised herself to stay away from him, in order to not hurt Asgar.

The look in Samuel's eyes was one of complete devastation. He was shaking his head, looking at her, mouthing, *How? How did this happen?*

Chapter 12

I SPENT most of the day on the phone talking to what felt like everyone in the county who had to do with my son's education or just education in general. No matter who I got ahold of, they all said the same thing.

He was going to Fishy Pines. It was already arranged, and he would start the coming Monday. It didn't matter how much I fought them or how angry I got or how much I threatened to write a book about them and their tyrannical ways. The decision was made, and it was *what was best for Victo*r.

I hung up and threw the phone on the couch with a loud cry. I grabbed my coffee cup and walked to the window. I looked out at Victor playing with his trees. He seemed to be so happy when he got to be outside.

Sophia came up next to me. She had been there most of the day, for moral support, she said.

"Maybe it's not such a terrible idea," she said and sipped her coffee. "Going to Fishy Pines."

"What do you mean?"

She shrugged. "Look at him. He's twelve, Emma. This

was fine when he was eight and maybe even when he was ten, but he's about to hit puberty. He'll be a teenager next year. I'm sorry to be the one to tell you but the boy is weird. There, I said it."

I looked at her, then back at Victor. I sipped some coffee while pondering what she had said. I knew she was right. Deep down, I knew the boy was strange and had known for all his life. He knew it himself too. I just didn't want him to have a label telling him he was sick. I never saw him as being sick. I saw him as being special. Different, but not in a bad way.

"Maybe they'll know how to open him up a little," Sophia continued. "You know, get him to use his skills, what makes him special. Like numbers. He's amazing with numbers."

"I fear they might drug him," I said.

"I don't think they can do that without your consent," she said.

"True. But I'm afraid I might give it to them. What if they persuade me with all their doctors' words and all that? I won't be able to say no, especially not if they somehow convince me it might help him. What if it does help him? I can't say no to that."

Sophia nodded. "I see what you mean. I'm sure it'll be fine. Heck, there are crazy people all over the world doing just fine. Just look at our mayor."

I laughed. "Lisa Rasmussen. Oh, yeah, that's one cuckoo head that's made it in this world."

We left Victor to play, and went back into the kitchen and finished our coffee.

"So, how was Maya this morning?" Sophia said.

I had told her about what happened, even though it was against Morten's advice. I needed to talk to someone about it and he was too busy. Besides, she was going to hear eventually once the media got ahold of the story of the boy found in the dunes if the rumors didn't beat them to it. So far, they had kept it a secret, but I had a feeling it wasn't going to be long before the island was crawling with journalists from the mainland. Asgar was, after all, the son of a very wealthy and well-known family, the Dragstedts. They were the owners of Fanoe Golf, the first golf course in Denmark, established in 1901, ranked fourth best in continental Europe.

As soon as they realized he had been killed, the media were going to eat the story up. And it wouldn't be long before it went public since I knew Morten was at the high school right now telling them the news, now that the family had been advised and were on their way back from their trip. After that, there would be no turning back.

Chapter 13

MAYA CAME HOME EARLY. Not that I was surprised. I was actually more surprised that she chose to go to school at all after what I had told her, but she said she needed to be there. For her friends.

She was crushed, and I grabbed her in my arms and held her tight for a very long time. Sophia had already left to go clean up her house. She had put Alma in daycare three days a week. She needed her out of the house to get all the housework done, but other than that, she enjoyed having her around, especially since she was the last one. Sophia had the doctor sterilize her to make sure of that.

"No more accidents," she said. "They're awfully cute but I simply can't afford them."

Maya sniffled and pulled out of my hug.

"Oh, Mom. It was awful. People were crying. They closed the school down for the day."

"Let me make you some hot chocolate," I said and walked into the kitchen. Maya followed me and sat down. She blew her nose in a tissue and then continued to cry. I heated some chocolate milk, then placed it in front of her and put whipped cream on it. I made one for myself and Victor too, then called for him to come inside.

"It's not the right time," he said.

"I don't care. Come in anyway. Your sister needs you."

He stood in the doorway. "But this is not when we have afternoon tea," he said, stomping his boots, causing snow to fall from them onto the carpet. "We always have afternoon tea with bread and jam at three o'clock. It is only one-thirty. This is not when we have our afternoon tea."

I sighed and rolled my eyes. "Maya needs us, Victor. Could we bend the rules a little for once? For her sake?"

"But it's not the right time."

"No, you're right."

"It is not right."

I exhaled. "I know. It's not. And it's not afternoon tea. It's just a cup of hot chocolate that has nothing to do with afternoon tea."

Victor paused. "So, we'll have afternoon tea at three?"

"Yes."

"And you'll bake?"

"Yes, I'll bake the bread you usually have."

"And I'll have two pieces of bread with jam on top of it."

"Yes."

Victor smiled. It was rare to see him do that. He didn't look at me when he did since he never looked at anyone he spoke to, but I could still see it.

"Now, can we go have hot chocolate?" I asked and closed the door to the freezing outside.

He didn't answer but rushed to the kitchen and sat down. He started to gulp down the hot chocolate.

"Whoa," I said, barely making it into the kitchen before he had emptied the cup and licked off the whipped cream from his upper lip.

"What's the rush?"

Maya didn't say anything. She sat with a spoon in her hand and twirled the whipped cream around, staring into her cup and sniffling.

"I have to get back," Victor said.

"It's not like the trees are going anywhere," Maya said, sounding a little more like herself.

"No, but Skye might."

I wrinkled my forehead. Victor stared at the tabletop.

"Who is Skye?"

"A girl," he said as he stood up and ran out.

My eyes met Maya's.

"A girl?" I asked.

She shook her head and sipped the hot chocolate. "Probably just one of his imaginary friends."

I drank from my cup and felt it warm me. It had been especially cold today and the old house had a hard time heating up properly.

"You're probably right," I said.

"Can I go to my room now?" Maya said after a few minutes' silence.

I looked at her, surprised. I had hoped she would stay and talk a little since there had to be a lot going on in that mind of hers.

"Sure. I won't keep you, but didn't you want to talk about what happened today? About Asgar? You must be feeling terrible."

Maya got up and walked to the door, then shrugged. "I'm okay. Maybe we can talk later."

Chapter 14

SHE WAS TRYING to do her homework, but couldn't focus. Her mind kept spinning, thinking about Asgar and what had happened to him. Still, she didn't want to talk to her mother about it. It wouldn't make her feel any better.

Christina had texted from the harbor when driving past it on her bike doing her paper route this afternoon. She said she had seen the massive amounts of reporters exiting the ferry coming from the mainland, invading the island. They all knew it was going to happen, especially since Asgar's family was quite well known in the country. She could only imagine them barricading their estate on the east end of the island and the reporters waiting for someone to come out and make some sort of statement.

Maya didn't know Asgar's family very well, but she had met both his mom and dad once when Asgar invited her to dinner. They were nice people and seemed kind and very polite, but also very cold towards Asgar. He had often told her how he never felt like he was good enough for them. He never fit properly into their world and who they wanted him to be, he said.

They had often talked about sending him to boarding school, much to Asgar's concern. He didn't want to leave his friends and knew he wouldn't make it in a boarding school environment. Maya knew he was right. Asgar was way too sweet. He was a sensitive type, and he loved to write. He had written her a poem once that she absolutely loved. He always told Maya how lucky she was to have a famous author for a mother…someone who would understand her desire to express herself, something his parents would never let him do. He was going to take over the family business of running the golf course and that was it. That was going to be his life. His parents' life was going to be his future. And nothing scared him more. Secretly, Asgar dreamt of becoming a reporter and eventually an author.

Maya sighed and leaned back in her chair, then she heard a sound outside her window. A small pebble hit the glass. She walked to it and opened it, a breeze of sheer cold hitting her face.

"Samuel?"

"I tried to text you. You didn't answer."

She glanced at her phone on the desk. She had turned it off after texting with Christina. She didn't want to talk to anyone today or be a part of the group chats where they were all speculating about Asgar's death and what happened to him. It had started immediately after the meeting at the gymnasium and already people were spreading rumors and speculations. Some believed Asgar had committed suicide while others wrote they thought he might have been attacked by aliens. It was ridiculous, and Maya didn't want to listen to any of it.

"Can I come in?" he asked.

Maya nodded. There was a ladder on the side of the house that he could use. She would ask him to use the front door but didn't want her mom to see him since she would just start to interrogate her about him and who he was and whether he might be her boyfriend, and Maya couldn't deal with all that right now.

Kenneth II growled as Samuel crawled through the window and Maya shushed him.

"Kenneth!"

She was so tired of that dog, but it was hers and she had to take care of him. She had a hard time even looking at the dog after her mom had told her that it had bit into Asgar's dead fingers. She kept imagining it. It was just too much. She sent him into the hallway and closed the door, so he couldn't get back in. He would probably destroy something, and then her mom would yell at her, but she didn't care.

Samuel sat on the bed. His eyes were red.

"I didn't want anyone to see me," he said. "That's why I didn't ring the doorbell."

"It's probably better this way," she said. "People talk around here. Especially my mom and her friend Sophia."

He nodded with a sniffle. Maya handed him a tissue from the package. She had created a pile of used ones on the desk.

"So…why are you here?" she asked and sat down next to him on the bed, careful not to touch him.

"I couldn't stand being at the house, at my home. I used to hang out with Asgar all the time. Everything at my house reminds me of him. Heck, everything in this town reminds me of him. I can't go anywhere without thinking about him and all the things we've done together."

Maya sighed deeply. "I know what you mean. I don't know how to go to school tomorrow, knowing he's not there. Who's gonna make me laugh through Mrs. Holm's boring math class? He always makes these grimaces behind the teacher's back and it makes me laugh so hard." Maya paused. "Or…he did…I mean he used to."

She pressed back tears. Samuel chuckled at a memory.

"Or the little notes he would send to someone behind him and get them in trouble?" Samuel said. "That always made me laugh."

"Me too."

"And when he would make fun of Camille and the other popular girls by acting like a mime."

Samuel laughed. "That's always a good one. Oh, how annoyed she would get at him for walking right behind her as she strode across the cafeteria, him mimicking her every move. That was precious. He is quite the actor." Samuel stopped himself, then looked up at Maya. "I mean…was."

There was a silence. Samuel broke it.

"How do you think he died?"

She shook her head. "I don't know. All I know is he was found in the dunes. It was actually my dog that found him. My mom was walking him when he found the body."

"Geez," Samuel said.

"Do you think he was killed?" Maya asked.

Samuel shrugged. "It kind of sounds like he was, right?"

"But who would kill him?" Maya asked. "Who on earth would want to see sweet Asgar dead?"

Samuel bit his lip. "That's actually partly why I'm here. I think his dad might."

Chapter 15

SHE WAS FEELING WEAK. Susan was having a hard time staying awake. He had been draining her blood. The weird figure with the mask had pumped blood out of her body every day, using his equipment in the room. Susan knew that was why she felt so feeble, but she couldn't do anything about it, no matter how much she struggled, she couldn't move. She had tried to talk to him, to ask him what he wanted from her, why she was there, but she couldn't say anything because of the gag, and she had a feeling that even if she did manage to speak and even if he did hear her, he wouldn't have answered.

He didn't speak to her while he worked around her; all she heard was him whistling inside the mask.

Now he was coming back. She could hear his footsteps approaching and see the door handle move.

Please, don't take any more of my blood, she thought to herself, shivering.

The man with the peeling skin had something between his hands this time. It looked like a tray. He placed the tray on top of her and pushed a button to lift the head of the bed and help her sit up. Soup and bread were on the tray. Susan gasped behind the gag. She was so hungry she felt like she could die. And thirsty. So terribly thirsty.

The man leaned over and took off her gag, a part of his scaly skin landing on top of her covers. Susan felt sick and wanted to wipe it off, but couldn't move. She moved her jaw as the gag was removed, then let out a loud scream.

That made the masked man laugh. He sounded like Darth Vader when he spoke and breathed behind the mask.

"You can scream all you want to, little girl, no one can hear you out here," he said once she ran out of air.

She groaned in anger and tried to move her hands, but still couldn't. The masked man leaned over and served her some soup on a spoon. Susan refused to open her mouth.

The man tried again. "You gotta eat, my precious," he said. "Gotta feed those delicious blood cells of yours."

She stared at him, wondering who was behind that black mask and why he was wearing it. It couldn't be just so she wouldn't see his face. He could have worn any mask for that. This seemed like a special one, designed specifically for some purpose that he needed it for.

"Eat, girl," he said and urged the spoon forward.

She took the spoonful, unable to resist it any more.

"That's my girl," he said, then hurried up and gave her another one. It felt good to get something to eat. Susan looked at the many watches in front of her, looking like they were mocking her, telling her how much time she had spent in captivity. It was almost midnight. Just like the night before when he came to her.

"That's good," he said and put the tray down when she had finished the soup and bread. He then gave her water to drink and she gulped it down greedily. He approached the hospital equipment and took out another long needle just like the one he had used the night before. It was attached to a tube that fed her blood into bags.

"Oh, no," she said, crying while he approached her holding the needle up. "Please. Not again. I can't lose any more blood. Please. PLEASE!"

Part II
ONE WEEK LATER

Chapter 16

SHE WAS LOOKING at the empty chair in the middle of the classroom. Actually, there were two of them now and it had Maya deeply worried. Not only was Asgar's chair empty, but so was Susan Ludvigsen's. And it had been for over a week now, maybe even more.

Normally, Maya wouldn't have noticed if Susan wasn't in school since she was known to skip class a lot with her boyfriend, Caspar, who was in the other class down the hall. The two of them liked to experiment with drugs and alcohol, and everyone knew about it, so no one worried if they went on a bender for a few days. It was almost expected.

But since Asgar's death, empty chairs in the classroom had Maya worried.

She approached Samuel about it between classes, when she met up with him in the hallway to go to the lunchroom.

"Susan is missing too. Susan Ludvigsen from my class. She's been gone for at least a week, if not more," she said. "I'm scared something has happened to her."

The two of them had been talking a lot lately, especially after Samuel had told her everything he knew about Asgar's family. He had told her Asgar had come to him a few weeks before he was found dead and told him he was considering running away. He was scared of his father, he said. He had never told Samuel what it was he was so afraid his father might do or why he was afraid of him since Asgar had told him it didn't matter; the less he knew the better. But now he wished he had asked more about it. Samuel felt so helpless because he felt like he could have prevented his death. Maya told him he probably couldn't have, but she understood his concern.

"Isn't she that drug-head? The one who hangs out with Casper and does all those mushrooms and stuff?"

"Yes, and normally I wouldn't assume anything bad had happened, but after what happened to Asgar, I'm more worried."

"I'm sure she's fine," Samuel said as they walked into the lunchroom and sat at their usual table.

They opened their lunchboxes. Maya sighed when she saw a note from her mother saying, *Remember, I love you and I am here for you when you want to talk. Anytime. Kiss, Mom.*

Samuel chuckled while biting down on his apple. "Another one, huh?"

"Yes. It's every day now. She thinks I'm going into some depression or something. She's so worried about me. She says it all the time. I try to tell her I'm fine."

Samuel chewed. "Are you fine?"

Maya sighed. "I don't know. Maybe not."

He shook his head. "Yeah, me either. I keep expecting Asgar to walk up to our table and say something funny."

Maya chuckled. "Me too. I really miss him."

Christina came and sat with them. They got quiet.

Maya couldn't help still feeling guilty for hanging out with Samuel, even though Asgar wasn't there anymore. It was silly, she knew that, but she couldn't help herself.

"What are you two conspiring about?" Christina asked.

That was when Susan's mother entered the cafeteria.

Chapter 17

"YOU MUST BE VICTOR, welcome. My name is Hans-Peter, but you can call me HP. Most kids here do."

The man in front of me had told me he was a doctor, but he didn't look like one. He wasn't wearing a white coat with pens stuck in the front pocket nor did he hold a clipboard or a notepad or wear glasses that he would place on the tip of his nose when you said something wrong.

This guy was tall and fairly handsome. He was blond and had blue eyes and was wearing a knitted sweater and jeans. He looked mostly like a schoolteacher, which pleased me immensely. I didn't want Victor to feel like a patient.

Victor didn't look up at him and didn't shake the hand he was holding out in front of him.

"I'm sorry," I said. "Victor doesn't look at people when they talk to him nor does he like to be touched."

The doctor removed his hand. "That's perfectly fine. He doesn't have to. Hey, Victor, what do you say we go and take a look at the classroom?"

We followed him inside. "Victor used to work with this

therapist, Ole Knudsen, maybe you know him? He did some excellent work with him and got really far. Victor loved him, didn't you, buddy?"

The doctor turned around and looked at us, then smiled. "That's good. Good."

He opened the door to a classroom where four kids were sitting on a carpet, reading. It was nothing like what I had imagined. There were no kids screaming or pulling their hair out, no crazy eyes or pointing fingers. The other kids looked up. The teacher, a woman in her forties, short and slightly chubby, approached us, smiling from ear to ear, reaching out her hand.

"I'm Victoria Kristensen. I'll be Victor's teacher. Hello there, Victor. You ready to learn? I bet you are. Come with me."

My heart sank as this woman took my son away. He didn't seem hesitant though, nor did he seem frightened by this place. Maybe Sophia had been right, I thought to myself. Maybe it wasn't so bad after all?

HP closed the door to the classroom and then turned toward me. He showed me into his office where we sat down on couches. It all seemed very cozy and nice.

"Now, we don't like to refer to our kids as ill, sick, mentally ill or disturbed, or anything like that. The kids we have here are special. They have some very strong sides to them that we would like to nurture and then help them on the issues where they are not so strong. Like in Victor's case, we need to work on his social skills. He will be in a classroom with very few children because we believe that way it will be less overwhelming for him. He will learn to cooperate with these other children and hopefully communicate with them. Those are our goals. I see in his papers that he suffers from anxiety as well, which is very normal in children who are special like him. It is something we're very used to coping with, using breathing techniques and meditation."

I was baffled, to say the least. My jaw would have dropped, had I been a cartoon character. I couldn't believe what this man was saying to me, how he was approaching this entire issue. It was all I had ever dreamt of for Victor. Finally, someone understood that my child wasn't sick; he didn't need to take pills or be locked up because of who he was.

"So, what do you say?" HP said and threw out his hands.

"I…I have to say, I am surprised. I had prepared all kinds of strange things to say and ask and to be all defensive because I assumed you would accuse me of not having taken proper care of him and then I would have made a joke about Fishy Pines and something fishy around here, to break the tension, but I don't really need to, do I?"

HP stared at me. He wasn't blinking. Then he laughed.

"That was a good one, Fishy…something smells…yes, that would have broken the ice in case there was some, but I don't think we need it. About the name, it's called Fishy Pines because it was founded back some hundred years ago by a fishing family whose son watched his best friend be taken by the ocean. They were out on his father's boat. The son never was himself again, and one day he hung himself in their backyard. The mother felt so guilty because she felt like she should have helped him more. So, she started this place. To help kids like him. She managed to gather enough money by getting the Dragstedt family to invest, and so this place was built. It's an old building, you'll have to forgive that; it is in dire need of some renovation, but I'm sure Victor will be just fine here. Actually, I have a feeling he is going to do wonderfully. He looks like a great kid. Now, is there anything else you'd like for me to know about him? Otherwise, we'll take the problems as they come. I can't wait to get to know your special son, Miss Frost. I simply can't wait."

Chapter 18

"SUSAN!"

Susan's mom strode across the cafeteria. All eyes were on her skinny body, each and every one of the spectators wondering if the woman was drunk as usual. She had to be, didn't she? To burst into the school like this and start yelling?

It was common knowledge that Susan's mother, Charlotte Ludvigsen, had been drinking heavily ever since she lost her husband, who ran away with Trine Jensen from the Shell gas station by the harbor, the one with the curly blonde hair and very big breasts. If she was drinking before he left or if he left because she drank, most people didn't know. But they did know that Charlotte Ludvigsen soon lost her job as a nurse and had to go on welfare. She was mostly known to hang out behind Netto, Nordby's biggest downtown grocery store, along with the homeless and the other drunks. There, they could drink beers and smoke cigarettes all day long, while life passed them by.

"Where are you, Susan?"

Mrs. Ludvigsen's eyes searched the cafeteria till they fell

on the social pariahs' table in the far corner, where a red-eyed Caspar was eating his lunch. He stopped chewing as their eyes met across the room.

"You!" Mrs. Ludvigsen yelled and walked towards him, pointing her finger at the boy.

He looked confused. Every student in the lunchroom had stopped eating and was staring.

"You!" she yelled and closed in on him. "Where is my daughter? Where is Susan?"

Caspar shook his head. "I…I don't know."

"Liar! You expect me to believe that? Tell me where she is. I need to talk to her."

"I…I really don't know where she is."

"Liar," she repeated. "Where is she? She hasn't been home all week."

Caspar looked perplexed. Maya's eyes met Samuel's and she felt her heart drop.

"I don't know. I swear," Caspar said. "I haven't seen her all week. I thought she was at home. She hasn't answered any of my calls or texts. I thought she was angry with me. I'm the one who should be angry. She just left me there on the beach."

"She what?" Mrs. Ludvigsen asked.

"We were on the beach last week. I think it was Thursday? Maybe it was Wednesday? Monday. It was on a Monday…I think. I don't remember, but we were hanging out and having…fun and then she was suddenly gone. I heard her yell that she was going home or something. That she wasn't feeling so well." He shook his head. "I don't know. She was just gone."

Mrs. Ludvigsen shifted on her feet. "You mean to tell me you don't know where she is? That she hasn't been with you all week? I thought she was hiding out with you at your place doing…whatever it is the two of you do together, which I have a feeling isn't homework."

Caspar rubbed his forehead. He was sweating, and it wasn't even warm in the cafeteria. Maya felt Samuel's hand in hers, he was squeezing it tightly.

Chapter 19

WITH VICTOR GONE ALL DAY, I suddenly had time to get some writing done. I was so happy to have him out of the house and, on top of, it in a place where I believed he would be understood, where they got him and who he was. Maybe they could even teach me something about him and how to better handle him. All I really wanted was for them to teach him how to take care of himself. I wanted him to be independent, to be able to live as ordinary a life as possible.

I sat down at the computer and started to write. I felt inspired by the finding of Asgar's body and had started to write a little about it, not really knowing where it would take me. But today, I managed to write two more pages of what I hoped might become my next book and I felt really good about myself as the afternoon approached and I had to go bake the bread I knew Victor would crave—no, make that *demand*—once he got home. I wasn't even supposed to pick him up from the place (I still didn't know what to call it, institution didn't seem right, so I decided on school because that's what I called it when speaking to Victor.)

No, they would bring him home as they did with all the other children who only came for the school.

Just as I had put the bread in the oven, Sophia came over as usual for a cup of coffee before the kids came home from school. Alma was with her today and the girl ran into the living room and played with the Duplos while us big girls had a chat in the kitchen. I told her how excited I was about Fishy Pines, and the doctor, and the kids and she was very happy for me.

"I have a really good feeling about this place," I said and grabbed the cookie jar and served it to her. She dug in and so did I, feeling like I deserved it after all that I had accomplished lately.

"And I have started writing again," I said, crumbs dropping from my lips and landing on the counter.

"Really? That's great news," Sophia said. "I'm happy for you. Looks like things are back on track then? Can we talk about the murder of Asgar Dragstedt, then?"

I nodded. "Yes. Okay, so here's the deal. Latest news is that they say his entire body was drained of blood."

"What?"

"Yes, creepy, right?" I shivered, wondering why anyone would drain a body of blood. It had been the cause of death, the autopsy said. It hadn't reached the news yet, but Morten had told me.

"Extremely creepy." Sophia looked at her cookie, then put it down like she suddenly felt sick.

"But that's why the body looked so strange…like it had been in the ground for a very long time, but it hadn't. Just for a few days. Morten told me—even though he's not allowed to, so lips sealed—"

Sophia signaled that hers were sealed and she threw away the key.

"—that Asgar had a fight with his parents just before

they were supposed to leave for the skiing trip and decided he wasn't going to go this year, even though it has been a tradition ever since he was a young boy. But this year, he didn't want to go, so they left without him."

Sophia's eyes grew wide. "So, he was home alone when it happened?"

"Yes. The parents didn't hear from him all week, but they assumed he was angry with them after their little dispute. So, that's why they didn't report him missing. They didn't know."

Sophia bit down on a cookie. She looked speculative. "That's a little fishy if you ask me."

"Maybe. Maybe not. Maybe they were afraid to appear weak, you know how rich folks like that are, plus the boy was seventeen. He was almost a grown man."

"Still," Sophia said. "If it were Maya, you wouldn't just leave her. And even if you did, you would have been very worried when you called her and she didn't answer her phone. You would have done everything to find her, to talk to her, even if she was upset, wouldn't you?"

I nodded. Sophia made a good a point. "I sure would. But not all parents are the same."

Chapter 20

FISHY PINES HAD a small minivan that they used to transport the children back to their homes. I waited outside as it drove up in front of my house, my heart in my throat. The tip of my nose was turning into a Popsicle and my fingertips were hurting from the cold. I spotted Victor as the doors hissed open. He walked down the steps, then right past me.

"Have him ready at seven-forty tomorrow morning," the bus driver yelled at me before closing the doors and taking off.

"Okay," I yelled back, then hurried after Victor, who was already in the hallway. "Hey! Wait up, buddy."

I closed the door behind me and felt the warmth embrace me. Victor had thrown his backpack down and was already sitting in the kitchen, still wearing his winter suit.

"You're not taking that off?" I asked.

"It's time for afternoon tea," he said, looking down at his plate. "It's past three o'clock. Where is Maya? She should be here. She's always here when we have afternoon tea."

I looked at the clock on the oven. Victor was right. Maya was running late.

"Where is my bread?" Victor said.

"Coming right up," I said and cut two pieces of my warm freshly baked bread, then put strawberry jam on both of them and placed them in front of him. He started to eat.

"So, how was it?" I asked, excited yet slightly nervous.

He didn't answer. He ate.

"Come on, Victor. How was the new school?"

He shrugged.

"Did you like the teacher?"

He nodded.

"And the other kids, were they nice?"

He nodded again.

"What did you do?"

Victor rose to his feet and headed for the door.

"Hey," I said.

He stopped, hand still on the door handle. He didn't turn around, just stood there like he was frozen.

"Where are you going?"

"To the backyard," he said. "To be with Skye."

I smiled. He was really into this girl. Even if she was imaginary—like most of his friends were—it was the first time he had hung out with a girl. I wondered if it was part of the fact that he was growing older and would soon be hitting puberty. Was he practicing being around girls this way?

I'd have to talk to HP about it. He had told me they would like to spend the first week evaluating Victor and letting him settle before they would call me in for a talk about setting goals for him and how to best approach him. I liked that they didn't rush into things. They took their time and that was good for Victor.

"Can I go now?"

I smiled. "Of course, sweetie. Go, have fun."

Chapter 21

I WATCHED Victor in the yard for a little bit, while drinking my coffee and eating my bread, since Maya hadn't returned yet. I was getting slightly worried about her. Not something I would usually be, since she and her friends often would go downtown and have a bite to eat before coming home, but since finding Asgar in the dunes, I was a little uneasy at the thought of her running around on her own.

I texted her while sitting on the couch in my living room, asking her where she was, trying to sound all cheerful and not at all like the worried mom I was in reality.

She didn't text me back and now my heart was pounding. Could something have happened to her? I walked to the kitchen and looked outside into the street. It got dark early this time of year, and she knew she had to be home before then if she didn't want me to completely freak out.

I poured myself another cup of coffee, then decided I needed to calm down. I sat down with the local newspaper that was filled with the story of Asgar's death and how the police still had no new clues.

I called Morten, thinking if anything bad had happened anywhere on the island, he would know.

"Hi, babe. Nice to hear your voice," he said, picking up.

He sounded cheerful. That was a good sign.

"You too. How are things at work? Busy today?"

He exhaled. "Well, no more than usual lately. We have all these people from Copenhagen here still to help with the investigation and they do take up space, but they're nice people, so we'll get by."

He was being friendly. I knew he was annoyed at them. It was always the same when the teams came out from the capital to help. They didn't understand the island mentality and hated how slowly things went here. They needed it to be a snap and for people to be efficient. Plus, they looked down on Morten and his colleagues for being small town cops out here in the boonies. On top of that, the police station was really small and they didn't have enough desks for everyone, so that meant Morten and his colleagues had to sit wherever they could and were pretty much reduced to coffeemakers and treated like interns by the big shots from Copenhagen. I knew he hated it, but he was trying to keep a good tone. I respected him for that.

"What's wrong?" Morten said. "You sound upset."

He knew me so well. I sighed and bit a nail. "Maya hasn't come home from school yet."

"Ah, I see, and normally you wouldn't worry, but since…wait a minute," Morten said.

I could hear yelling on the other end.

"What's going on?" I asked.

"I need to talk to someone now," a distant voice yelled, sounding alarmingly desperate. "My daughter is missing!"

"I gotta go, Emma," Morten said.

"But…?"

"I'll call you later, okay?"

"Okay," I said, but he had already hung up on me. I stared at the phone, my heart pounding, my throat feeling tight.

Someone's daughter is missing!

As I stared at the phone, it suddenly started to ring. It was Maya. I felt a huge relief and picked it up.

"Where are you?"

"Easy, Mom. I'm fine."

"What's going on?"

She went quiet. "Someone is missing. A girl from my class. Susan Ludvigsen. She's been gone for a week or so, but her drunken mother didn't notice until now. We've been out searching for her on the beach, me and my classmates."

I sat down. "Oh, dear God."

"I know. It's bad," she said. "I'm scared."

Chapter 22

AS DARKNESS FELL upon the town, we all formed a search party. My neighbors Sophia and Jack joined in, along with most of the parents from the high school. Even my mom and dad joined in and took Victor with them. Victor loved spending time with my dad. Meanwhile, I had brought both Kenneth and Brutus. I figured since Kenneth had found Asgar, maybe he could help us find Susan too, only this time I would prefer her to be alive.

We walked the beach areas for hours, searching every dune, calling her name, and looking behind all the bushes and lush landscape. We shone our flashlights into all the small summer cabins that were usually vacant at this time of year, knocking on the windows and calling for her, in case she had crashed in one after getting high or drunk. Susan was known by everyone as quite the party girl, and I hoped and prayed that she had just partied a little too hard this time or maybe still was partying somewhere. Like her mother, she could go off on a bender for days in a row.

"A-a-anything?" Jack asked as he came up to me.

I shook my head. I had just looked inside my third cabin, but it was just as empty as the rest of them.

"No sign of her anywhere. I just wish we could get inside these cabins, you know, to search them properly."

"If we c-c-can't get in, then s-s-she can't either," he said.

His stuttering had gotten a lot better the past years. I was glad to see that he was making progress since it was a problem for him, one that often kept him from socializing with the rest of us. Jack was such a great guy. A bit of a loner because of the stuttering and because he took care of his sick sister who demanded his attention constantly.

"You're probably right," I said and left the porch of the wooden cabin. The wind was howling outside, and my cheeks were freezing. I couldn't help thinking there was no way Susan could be outside in this cold weather. If she was in this area, she had to be sheltered in one of the summer cabins along the beach.

I saw a sea of flashlights flickering in the darkness ahead of me and could hear many voices calling her name. Where could a seventeen-year-old girl disappear to? Had she left the island? I had called Morten earlier to tell him we were all coming down to the police station to help with the search, and he told me he had talked to the personnel on the ferry and to Linda, who sold the tickets down there. No one had seen Susan.

"And Linda would know," he said. "She knows everyone around here, plus she has a son in Susan and Maya's class. She would notice if Susan had bought a ticket or entered the boat."

Jack and I walked to the next summer cabin that was a lot bigger than the ones surrounding it. I shone my light through the window into a spectacular living room with high vaulted ceilings. It looked just as dark and empty as the rest of them.

"Susan!" I called. "Susan, are you in there?"

Jack shone his flashlight into another of the windows, then shook his head, returning to my side. I could hear Sophia yelling somewhere in the darkness. She couldn't stay out much longer since her mother couldn't look after her kids past nine o'clock.

"N-n-o one is h-ere," Jack said.

I exhaled and turned to walk away when suddenly the door to the cabin opened and a face peeked out. Kenneth started to growl as a figure appeared in the doorway.

"Who's there?"

I shone my flashlight at him. Kenneth barked. I pulled him back. The man in the doorway was very old and his face and hands were wrinkled. He was pale but had unnaturally red lips.

"I am so sorry, sir," I said. "We thought the cabin was empty. I didn't know anyone was here. We're looking for a girl, her name is Susan Ludvigsen. Here. This is her."

I showed him a picture of her from my phone. Charlotte Ludvigsen had sent it to all of us.

"Have you seen her around here?"

The old man looked down at the picture, putting his glasses on, then shook his head.

"Never seen her before."

"All right, but if you do, please call the police station. We are all searching for her."

"Of course," the old man said. "What a terrible tragedy. So young and such a pretty face."

"Yeah, well…we still hope to find her alive."

"Oh, good. Let's hope you do, then."

Jack and I left his porch, me with an uneasy feeling in my stomach.

"M-maybe we should have knocked first," he said.

"I know," I said. "We'll do that from now on. But in our defense, the house looked empty like the rest of them. I never thought anyone would be here at this time of year. These are all summer residences. People don't usually come out here in January. Plus, who on earth sits inside a dark house? Why hadn't he turned on any of his lights?"

Jack chuckled. "Maybe he was asleep."

"Or maybe he's a vampire," I joked, "and just sits there in the darkness waiting for his victims to come by."

Jack chuckled again. "T-that's why you're the best-selling author and I am n-not," he said.

We walked on, Kenneth pulling on the leash, Brutus trotting along behind me, being so silent I almost forgot he was there. I needed no leash for him because he always stayed close to me, unlike Kenneth, whom I didn't trust not to run off without a leash anymore. My heart couldn't stop beating fast when I thought about my joke and the fact that Asgar's body had been drained of blood. Who would do such a thing? Who in their right mind killed someone by draining them of their blood?

Chapter 23

SOPHIA LEFT us just before nine, when my parents also caved in and said they would go back to my house and stay there with Victor till I got back. My mom was getting frostbite on her face, she said as she shivered. I was about to make a comment about the way she had dressed in high heels and just a light jacket but then decided against it.

Jack and I continued for yet another hour, when we too had to give in to the cold and the fatigue. We walked across the beach till we could see my house from the ocean side, warm lights gleaming from inside of it. This house always made me so happy. At the end of my yard, Jack gave me a hug goodbye and left to go home to his own house. I walked up the yard, Kenneth pulling me ahead, Brutus right behind me.

As we walked between the tall trees I looked up at them, wondering how long they had been here and how much they had seen. I had grown to love those trees almost as much as Victor did. At first, when we moved in, I had considered cutting them down since they blocked a big part of the view of the ocean from the house, but once I realized how much Victor loved them, there was no way I could do that. Now, I couldn't believe I had even thought about it. The trees were gorgeous. So magnificent, almost royal.

Kenneth was pulling forcefully as we approached the house, probably dreaming about the warmth and coziness just like I was at this point, when suddenly, Brutus made a sound.

Everything stopped. Brutus was always silent. He never made a sound. Yes, one deep bark had come out of his mouth. I gasped and turned around. He had stopped at a tree and was looking up at it.

"What is it, Brutus?" I asked and approached him.

Had this been Kenneth, I wouldn't have lifted an eyebrow since he barked and growled at everything and especially at trees if there was a bird or a squirrel in them, or maybe just because he could. But this was Brutus. This was the big silent dog that never ever made a sound even when he walked, even if a squirrel jumped right down in front of him. Not even the neighbor's cat could get his attention, but this had. Something was up in that tree and he needed me to see it.

I walked closer and patted Brutus on the head. "What's up there, buddy? What did you see?"

The dog didn't move. He was still staring up at the branches and now I saw it too. On top of one of the thick branches sat a girl.

"What the…?"

I shone my flashlight at her. She was sitting on top of the branch, barely holding on, her legs dangling.

I stared at her, startled. "What are you doing up there, little girl?"

She tilted her head. Her long hair was messy and her face dirty.

"Come down here before you fall and hurt yourself."

Much to my amazement and terror, the girl let go of the branch and jumped. Just like that.

I panicked and let out a loud scream. But in the same second, I realized I didn't need to be afraid. The girl wasn't falling. She wasn't heading towards the ground, head first. She was floating right above me, her face grinning. She stayed like that, hovering above me, for what felt like minutes but was probably just seconds. I couldn't breathe. I watched her make a summersault in the air, then land in front of me, feet first in the snow.

Chapter 24

MY MOM and dad were sitting together on the couch, holding hands when I entered from the yard, the girl right behind me, trotting along with Brutus. Kenneth ran to my dad and growled at him, making him laugh.

"Emma?" My mom said, concerned. "Who is the girl?"

I shrugged. "I don't know."

I closed the door behind us and took off my snow-covered boots and my jacket. I stared at the girl, who was shivering with cold. I grabbed a blanket from the couch and wrapped her in it.

"I found her in the yard, sitting in a tree," I said to my mom.

"You did what? But...how? Where did she come from? Where are her parents?"

I sighed, annoyed. "I don't know, Mom. Yet."

"She needs something warm, she must be freezing," she said. "I'll make some herbal tea."

"How about some hot chocolate instead?" I said. "She might like that a little better."

My mom looked dissatisfied, then nodded. "All right then."

The girl stared at the living room, eyes big and a little frightened. "Go on, sit down," I said and pointed at the couch next to my dad. "We'll get you warmed up real fast."

My dad smiled like the gentle giant he was. I rushed to my mom in the kitchen to make sure she didn't make some tasteless organic non-fat, non-dairy chocolate milk with soy instead of sugar.

"Where on earth did this girl come from, Emma?" she asked.

"I don't know. I told you she was sitting in the tree outside, freezing like crazy."

"What's her name?"

"I don't know."

"Have you even asked her?"

I sighed, annoyed. My mom had a way of sounding like she blamed me for everything. "I have, but she didn't answer. She just stares at me with those big green eyes of hers like she doesn't understand."

"That's odd."

"You ain't seen half of it," I said.

My mom paced to the fridge and peeked inside. "Where's your almond milk?"

"I guess I ran out. Use normal milk," I said.

My mom grumbled something I knew I didn't want to hear, so I blocked it out. With the milk in her hand, she turned toward me.

"Why was she out there? At this time of night? Where are her parents?"

"I don't know," I said. "As I just told you, she hasn't said anything. I just hurried to get her inside before she froze to death."

My mom put the chocolate powder into the milk and

stirred while staring at the box of Nesquik. "Oh, dear, I didn't know it had that much sugar in it. Do you drink this stuff...you don't...do you? You give this to the kids?"

"Yes, Mom. I let my kids have sugar every now and then, big surprise."

She put the cup in the microwave and turned it on. "No need to take a tone with me."

I exhaled. "I'm not. But come on, Mom, a little sugar every now and then won't hurt them."

She gave me a look that immediately saddened me. I knew how she felt about me, I knew she was thinking, *maybe not them, but you.* I knew she thought I had gotten fat and that I needed to be more careful. And I knew she was right. I just wasn't very good at it.

The microwave dinged, and my mom took out the cup. As she was about to leave with it in hand, I stopped her. I grabbed the whipped cream and put in a big clump.

"There. Now it's perfect."

My mom looked at me like I was crazy, then shook her head and left. I followed behind her. Inside the living room, we saw my dad and the girl. He had found Victor's old chess game and had set it up. He looked at us when we approached him.

"She's really good," he said with a chuckle.

I smiled and sat down. The girl looked at her hot cocoa and used the spoon to shovel it into her mouth. Then she smiled, whipped cream stuck to her upper lip.

"That's great, Dad," I said. "It really is, but now we need to talk to her for a little while, and try and find out how we can help her."

"What is your name, little girl?" my mom took over.

The girl tilted her head like she had done when she was up on the branch looking down at me.

"Oh, dear Lord," my mom said. "It's like she's a cave

person. She doesn't understand what I'm saying, does she?"

"Maybe she's a tourist," my dad said. "My guess would be German. Sprechen Sie Deutsch?" he asked. "No? How about English? Or what about Swedish? Pratar ni svenska?"

Still, the girl only stared at him, her pretty eyes blinking.

"Skye?"

It was Victor. He was standing in the doorway, still in his PJs. For once, he was looking up and not at his feet when speaking.

I stood up with a light gasp. "This is Skye?" I chuckled, relieved. "Of course, it is. It's her."

Victor approached us. "What is she doing in here?"

"She was freezing outside, Vic," I said. "If I hadn't brought her inside, she would have frozen to death."

"She sleeps in the shed," he said. "I gave her blankets and pillows and everything."

"So, this is Skye," I said. "Huh. Does she have a last name?"

Victor shrugged. "I don't know. I call her Skye because she fell from the sky one day while I was in the yard."

"She what?" my mother asked.

"She jumped down from a tree, just like she did to me," I said, leaving out the part where she had floated in the air above me for several seconds without falling.

"Oh."

"But, Victor," I said. "We need to find her parents. Do you know anything about her?"

Victor looked at the floor again. "I know that she can fly and that she is nice."

If it were humanly possible, my mother's eyes would have fallen out at this point. My dad grabbed her arm.

"You know Victor has a huge imagination," he said.

"Has she spoken to you, Victor? Has she said anything at all?" I asked.

"She speaks to me in my mind sometimes. She puts in a word or a picture."

"Oh, dear Lord. The boy is losing it," my mom said. "You need to take her to the police station. Have Morten search for her parents."

"Of course, I will, Mom, but for now I'm just trying to help her, okay?"

"Maybe we should go home. It's getting late," my dad said. He poked Skye lovingly on the shoulder. "I'll get my revenge next time, okay? Promise me a rematch?"

The girl didn't understand a word he said but gave him an endearing smile that made him laugh. He turned to Victor and put his hand on his shoulder. My dad was the only one who could touch my son without it ending in him screaming or throwing a fit.

"This one is special," he said. "She's a keeper, my boy. Don't you mess this up, you hear me?"

Chapter 25

MAYA and her friends didn't stop searching till ten thirty and the cold finally made them give up. She and Samuel walked together through town. They knocked on all the doors and asked if anyone had seen her, but so far, they had no luck.

She and Samuel rode their bikes home and he followed her up to her front door.

"I'm sorry," he said. "That we didn't find her."

"Yeah, me too."

He went silent for a few seconds. "Do you think her disappearance had anything to do with what happened to Asgar?"

"It's quite odd that it should happen right at the same time as his body appeared, isn't it?"

Samuel nodded. Maya looked at his perfect skin and glowing blue eyes. He was so handsome. Tall and muscular without being buff like some of the other boys at the high school.

"It sure is. I can't stop thinking about Asgar and his parents. After their fight, he told me he was going to run away. You think they might have killed him because of that?"

Maya wrinkled her forehead. "Probably not. Doesn't sound like something you'd kill your son over. Besides, his body was drained of blood, I heard Morten tell my mom. It doesn't sound like something someone would do because they were angry."

"Maybe they killed him because of what they were fighting about, then," he said.

"Do you know what it was?" Maya asked.

"No. But he told me he was afraid of his dad."

"I know they wanted him to take over the golf course once he grew up, but he would rather be a writer. That's what he told me. Could that be what they were fighting about?" Maya asked.

Samuel shrugged. "Sure. But would his dad threaten him because of that?"

"I don't know," Maya said. "How about we find out?"

"What do you mean?"

"I don't know. I feel so helpless, so useless. I never liked those parents of his. If they did something to him, then I want to know. Don't you?"

Samuel looked pensive, then nodded. "Sure. But how?"

"I know a little something about computers and getting into them. I've learned from my mother. Maybe if I get access to his?"

Samuel contemplated the idea for a few seconds, biting his lip. "That doesn't sound like such a bad idea."

Maya looked in through the kitchen window. "The lights are still on, so my mom is still up. Go around the back. If she sees you, I won't hear the end of it."

Samuel nodded. "Sure. No problem."

Maya grabbed the door handle while Samuel rushed

around the house. She walked inside. "Mo-om? Are you up?"

Maya walked into the living room where she found her mother and Victor and some girl she had never seen before. The girl was levitated above the couch.

"What is going on here?" Maya asked.

Her mother sighed and shook her head. She looked confused. "This is Skye. We found her in the backyard, don't ask."

"How? H-how is she doing that?"

"She can do a lot of stuff," Victor said, sounding unusually excited.

"We're taking her to the police station tomorrow, so they can find her parents," Maya's mom said.

The girl let herself drop onto the couch and laughed. Victor clapped his hands, then approached her. He gave her a hug. Maya stared, startled at her brother. Just when she didn't think he could get any weirder.

"Mom? He's hugging her. Victor is touching her? Touching a stranger? Touching another human being?"

Her mother exhaled. "I know. He's been acting very differently ever since she came into the house. Your grandfather thinks he's in love. I don't know what it is or who she is, but I'm beginning to think she might be Heaven-sent."

Maya heard the ladder bump against the side of the house and remembered Samuel.

"I-I'll be in my room," she said, walking backward towards the stairs. "And sleep. I'll be in my room...sleeping."

Chapter 26

VICTOR INSISTED that Skye sleep in his room. I wasn't sure I completely loved the idea, but he was so excited to have her close and I had to admit I had never seen him quite like this before. It had me thrilled too.

I put a mattress on the floor for Victor and he gave her his bed, much to my surprise since he never liked for things to change and not be the way they always were. He never liked to share anything that was his. That was why he never brought anything to share in class for his birthday.

I tucked them both in and sang a song before walking to the door where Brutus sat, ready for his bedtime, which seemed to consist of him just sitting there, staring at the kids while they slept. I realized I had never seen the dog actually sleep. Did he sleep?

"I'll leave it slightly ajar in case you need to go to the bathroom," I said, even though I knew Skye didn't understand a word I said.

I walked into the hallway and stood for a few seconds and listened. I couldn't stop wondering about the girl and it dawned on me that she had been in Victor's life for quite some time now. It was more than a week ago that he first mentioned her, and I had believed she was just a part of his imagination. Why hadn't anyone been looking for her? If she was a tourist, why wasn't anyone searching for her? I knew Morten would definitely have told me if a young girl was missing on the island. Everyone would know by now, just like everyone knew about Susan and was searching for her.

I looked out the window into the dark night, wondering about Morten, who was still out there searching for Susan. Did her disappearance have anything to do with Skye's sudden appearance? It had all happened within the past week or so.

Something odd was definitely going on.

I sighed and went downstairs to turn out the lights before going to bed. I spotted Skye's shoes in the hallway. Had she been living in our shed for an entire week? Or maybe even more? She must have been freezing, I thought to myself. It was a wonder she hadn't died out there.

The girl flies, Emma. She talks in Victor's head. She's not normal.

"Levitates," I said to my own reflection in the dark window. "And I don't know if she really speaks to Victor in his head or if he is just making it up."

I felt like calling Sophia and telling her everything, but it was too late, and the lights at her house across the street were out, so she was probably sleeping. How would I explain it to her? How was I going to explain it to Morten? I had to somehow. I had to figure out where her parents were. The girl seemed to be Victor's age, so she wouldn't be out here on her own. Maybe something happened to them? An accident?

I nodded and shut off the lights in the kitchen. Yes, maybe that was it. Her parents probably couldn't get to her for some reason, or maybe they didn't know she was here on the island.

I grabbed my phone and called Morten to say goodnight. He didn't pick up, so I left a message telling him I loved him and missed him and that I had something I needed to talk to him about tomorrow morning. Something important.

I hung up, then walked up the stairs past Maya's room, when I thought I heard a sound coming from behind the door. I stood for a few seconds and listened, but there didn't seem to be anything. No, Maya had said she was going to sleep, so of course, she was sleeping. It was probably just Kenneth being unruly again. Why couldn't that dog be a little more like Brutus? I shook my head, walked to my room, and shut the door.

Chapter 27

SHE WAS HOLDING HER BREATH. Samuel was sitting next to her at her desk, not making a sound. Maya could hear her mother stop outside in the hallway and their eyes met, Maya's finger reaching her lips to make sure he kept quiet. If her mom found him in there at this time of night, Maya would be grounded for weeks.

Finally, her mom moved on down the hallway and she heard the door slam shut to her bedroom. Maya breathed, relieved. She looked at Samuel and their eyes locked for a few seconds. Then they snickered. Not loudly, in case her mom heard it, of course.

"That was close," Samuel whispered.

"Sure was."

Maya tapped on the computer.

"So, who was that girl downstairs?" he asked.

Maya stopped. "You saw her?"

He nodded. "Through the window as I ran around the house."

Maya bit her lip. "D-d-id you see what she did?"

He nodded. "How did she do that?"

Maya swallowed. "I don't really know. It's very strange."

Samuel smiled. "I thought it was awesome."

"Really?" Maya felt happy. She feared Samuel would just think she was weird; it was always her fear that the outside world would realize how weird she and her family were, especially her brother. She was afraid of what they might say about her in school.

"So, you won't tell anyone if I ask you not to?"

"No. Of course not."

Maya tapped along, her fingers dancing on the keyboard. Samuel looked at her with admiration in his eyes. It made her blush.

"I'm in," she said and looked up at Samuel. He smiled.

"Awesome. I didn't know you could do that."

Maya shrugged. "It wasn't even hard."

"Not for you, maybe." Samuel focused on the screen. "So, now what? What can you find?"

"First, I'll go through all his emails to see if there's anything there," she said and opened Asgar's email account. It felt strange invading his privacy this way, even though he wasn't there anymore.

"So?" Samuel asked as she opened one email after another, most of it spam, but some private letters between him and his friends as well, nothing important, though.

"I don't seem to see anything out of the ordinary," I said.

"Let's try his Facebook," he said. "And Instagram."

Maya started with Instagram and they went through a ton of pictures and videos, but Asgar hadn't been very active in there himself, so it seemed useless. Maya then opened his Facebook and right away she found something of interest. Asgar had been writing back and forth with someone for quite some time. It was mostly him who had written her, whereas she had answered in short sentences.

"He was begging her to meet with him, why?" Samuel asked. He was getting closer to Maya, so close their arms brushed up against each other. Maya felt a warmth spread inside of her.

"I don't know," Maya said. "He doesn't say, only that it is important for him to meet with her, whereas she tells him she can't."

"Who is she?"

Maya clicked on the account. "She lives in Copenhagen," she said, baffled. "Why was he trying to meet with someone from Copenhagen?"

"Someone a lot older than him," Samuel said.

"That is odd." Maya leaned back in her chair.

Samuel looked at his phone. "It's getting late. I should be getting home before my mom starts to wonder where I am," he said as he leaned over and gave her a hug.

As he let go of her, they were face to face for a few magical seconds before he leaned forward and placed his lips on top of hers.

Chapter 28

I COULDN'T SLEEP. Of course, I couldn't. Who would be able to with all that was going on?

As the clock struck midnight and I still hadn't closed an eye, I got up and walked to my laptop. I sat down and stared at the screen for a few minutes, then started to write. I wrote about the girl, about Susan, and some more about Asgar and, so far, it didn't really make a lot of sense, but at least I got some words on paper as my mind kept circling about it and especially about the girl, Skye, who had "fallen" from the tree.

I walked to the window, then noticed the lights were on at Sophia's house. I grabbed my phone and texted her.

YOU UP?

The answer came swiftly. YES. ALMA HAS A FEVER.

I answered: I'M COMING OVER.

I ran downstairs, grabbed my jacket and boots, wrote a note for the kids in case any of them woke up, then I rushed across the street and entered Sophia's house.

She was sitting in the living room, Alma in her arms.

"She just fell asleep," she said.

"You want me to call Dr. Williamsen?"

She shook her head. "I already spoke to him. The fever isn't too bad. It's just a little cold. You know how kids get a fever from practically nothing."

"I vaguely remember," I said, realizing it had been a long time since I last had a toddler.

"So, what's going on?" Sophia asked while swaying back and forth to make sure Alma slept deeply. "Why aren't you sleeping? You usually sleep like a rock."

"A lot on my mind," I said. "Maybe we should talk tomorrow. You need your sleep."

"Are you kidding me? I'm not going to be able to sleep now. I never sleep when the kids are sick. I prefer to hold them in my arms, rocking them. That way, they sleep better, and she'll feel good tomorrow."

"You sure?"

"Absolutely. Having you here makes the night go faster, so you stay as long as you want to. What's going on?"

I sighed and rubbed my chin. "Victor has got a friend."

She looked surprised. "That's good, isn't it?"

"Yes, it's excellent, but she isn't a normal friend. She's not normal. In any way."

"Well…neither is Victor, so maybe that is a great thing. Did he meet her at the Pines?"

I shook my head. "No. That's the thing. He met her in our backyard. We don't even know her name, but we call her Skye because she—well she sort of fell from the sky."

"Fell from the sky? Because you don't know where she came from?"

I shook my head, feeling suddenly tired. "No, she actually fell from the sky."

"What?"

"She was in a tree, then jumped down...it's a long story. But no, we don't know where she's from."

"Can't you just ask her?"

"She doesn't speak, not a single word and she doesn't seem to understand what I say. But Victor says she speaks to him. She communicates...like through his thoughts. And, oh, yes...she flies, or I call it levitation; I don't know if it is actually flying."

Sophia stared at me. She blinked. "What?"

"I know it's late and all, but you heard me right. The girl can somehow get into the air and stay there."

"That sounds like the definition of flying to me."

I made a grimace. "It does, doesn't it?"

"What are you going to do?" Sophia asked.

"What do you mean?"

"As hard as it is to understand, and believe me I have a hard time really grasping what you're saying right now, so you might wanna repeat it sometime tomorrow—or even better—show it to me, but you have to figure out what to do."

"I was planning on taking her to the police station and talking to them. I figured they could help her."

"A girl like that?" Sophia said. "What if she suddenly starts to levitate inside the station? Do you even know if she can control when she does it and when she doesn't?"

"No. Not really."

"Does she realize it makes her weird?"

I shrugged. "I guess. I don't really know since she doesn't say a word."

Sophia sighed. "I think you should be very careful. What if they take her away and do experiments on her or something?"

"You really think they do stuff like that?"

"Of course. I have read a ton of stories online about people who were experimented on."

I sighed and rubbed my eyes. I was getting tired now. Sophia loved conspiracy theories a little too much for my taste and sometimes she would indulge in them. She even once told me she believed Fanoe Island had once been invaded by UFOs and that people around here talked about abductions and having experiments done on them during those abductions. I never bought into stuff like that, but I did fear she had a point. Skye risked ending up as a guinea pig somewhere or a circus freak on some TV show, and I already cared too much about the girl to let that happen. She had made my boy so happy and that was worth a lot in my book.

I walked home after saying goodnight to Sophia, wondering about what she had said, realizing that she was right. I had to be very careful how I handled this. As I approached my door, I heard a sound coming from the backyard, then rushed around the house to see what it was. I saw a shadowy figure disappear between the trees towards the beach. That was when I spotted the ladder leading to my daughter's bedroom window.

Chapter 29

HE WAS PUMPING blood from her again. Just like every other night. Just around midnight, he came to her room, fed her, and then started the pumping. Susan had a hard time staying awake anymore and slept most of the day away. And she was so thirsty all the time, so incredibly thirsty. She couldn't stand the sound of the many clocks ticking away, reminding her of how long she had been there.

"Tick-tock," the man with the mask said. "Boy, how time is flying, isn't it? Tick-tock."

Susan closed her eyes to not look at the blood gushing out of her into the tubes. She felt dizzy when looking at it and the thought of losing more made her certain that soon there would be no more left.

"Please," she mumbled and opened her eyes again, trying hard to stay awake, to stay conscious and not slip into the darkness she was terrified she would never come back from.

He had stopped gagging her since she was too weak to even scream. She kept slipping in and out of consciousness and he knew she didn't have long left. She would be running out of blood—and time—soon.

"Please, spare me."

She spoke almost in a whisper. The man hardly heard her. He didn't look at her and she closed her eyelids again, forced by their heaviness. A second later, she opened them, and that was when she saw it. The pair of scissors. He had carelessly placed them on the table next to her bedside. While he turned his back on her, she moved her fingers towards them, but couldn't reach them. She realized she could move slightly to the side if she wiggled her entire body to get herself closer. She reached out her pinky one more time, but still, it wasn't enough. Susan wiggled to the side again under the leather straps and came closer, closer still, and then almost had the scissors, when suddenly the masked man turned around and looked at her. She let her hand go dead and closed her eyes. He walked around her, pressing on the bag of blood.

"Almost there," he said satisfied, then walked back to the other side. "Just a few more drops."

Susan felt the drops leave her body, then opened her eyes a little, just enough to see that he had once again turned his back on her to polish his clocks. Cautiously, she reached out three of her fingers and managed to grab onto the handle of the scissors with her pinky and pulled them from the table onto the bed. It made a very small sound and she paused to make sure he didn't hear it.

He didn't. He was whistling *Waltzing Matilda* while polishing his old clocks, then he sang a line from it:

"And you'll come a-waltzing, Mati-i-i-lda, with me."

Susan pulled the scissors closer still, till she managed to pull them under the covers.

The man in the mask then turned his head and looked at her. He exclaimed, "That's it." He walked to the bag of blood, then looked at her. Susan kept as still as possible, her eyes closed.

"And you're still alive. Way to go, little girl. Guess we have at least a couple more portions coming from you. Gotta say, you have been good to me. Better than any of the others."

The masked man removed the tubes and cleaned up the blood that had dripped onto the floor, then left the room, whistling. He turned out the lights, then chirped, "Sleep tight, my princess, and remember what they say: *Blood is meant to circulate. Pass it around!*"

Part III

THREE DAYS LATER

Chapter 30

THE ENTIRE ISLAND was at the funeral. At least that was what it felt like. So many people came that it was hard to find a seat in the church. I went with Morten and Maya, while we left Victor at home with my mom and dad...and, of course, Skye. Sophia and Jack were there too, sitting next to Maya.

I introduced Skye to Morten on the day after she jumped into our lives. He came over for breakfast before work and saw her. I had allowed Victor to stay home and called the school to let them know he wasn't feeling well. So, he and Skye were sitting with me in the kitchen. I had baked cinnamon buns in my eagerness to make her feel at home, and she was eating as he walked in.

I meant to tell him about her, how I didn't know who she was or where she was from, I really did, but somehow, I couldn't get myself to do it. Morten was a police officer. He was a man of the law, and I knew he would alert the authorities and they would come and take her away from me, from Victor, and we would never see her again. If they never found her parents, she would become a number in the system, a system that wouldn't understand her or how to handle her.

So, instead, I told him she was visiting. That she was a child from Victor's new school and that she didn't speak; it was a part of why she was at Fishy Pines.

Morten was way too distraught to even question anything since his mind was with Susan Ludvigsen and her disappearance. He had been up most of the night before, so he didn't really care much about anything else.

The following evening when he came over and she was there again, I told him her parents were having a hard time and that I promised to have her for a little while. I felt awful for lying to him like that, but at the same time, I was terrified of what would happen to her if I was honest. I just had a feeling that I had to be very careful. Meanwhile, I had done my research and found all I could on missing children both here on the island and the rest of the country. It wasn't that hard since Denmark is pretty small. There was no one who matched Skye's description. No one seemed to miss her. So, there I was, keeping a flying girl in my house that I didn't know what to do about. It was probably very illegal, and on top of it, I was lying to my boyfriend.

Sitting in the church, I wondered if I had completely lost my mind.

"We're gathered here today to say goodbye to one of our island's dearest citizens," the pastor said as he started the ceremony.

People were already crying. The pastor then spoke about Asgar and how he had been a joy to his parents as a young boy. The pastor pointed at Mr. and Mrs. Dragstedt in the front, while speaking about the great tragedy of losing your child and how it wasn't God's will for him, but there were other forces on this earth, forces we allowed to rule here.

The door to the church squeaked open, the hinges complaining loudly, and everyone turned to see a woman come in, hurry to the pew behind us in the very back, then sit down.

Sophia made a noise that to me sounded slightly like a gasp.

"Who's she?" I asked.

"Leonora Dragstedt," Jack said.

"Dragstedt?" I asked.

Sophia nodded. She leaned forward to better be able to speak without being heard.

"Their daughter. Asgar's sister."

"I didn't know he had a sister. She's our age?"

Jack nodded. "I w-w-went to school with her. She disappeared b-before we graduated. Rumor has it she ran away. "

"With a boy," Sophia said.

"Someone the f-f-family didn't approve of," Jack said.

"Who was he?" I whispered.

"His name was Sven. Sven Evald. He came back to the island a few years later. Works down at the harbor."

"So, they're not together anymore?"

Sophia shrugged. "Probably not. My guess is she didn't want to come back after how they treated her."

"Or maybe they d-d-didn't want her back," Jack said. "After the scandal she created."

Chapter 31

MAYA CRIED and found it hard to keep herself composed. Once the ceremony was over, she walked outside following her mother. Asgar's parents were standing by the door to the church, greeting each and every person, thanking them for coming.

Maya stepped up and reached out her hand towards Mrs. Dragstedt. Her eyes were stern, her facial expression cold as a stone.

"I am so sorry for your loss," she said.

"Thank you, Maya," Mrs. Dragstedt said and took her hand. "Thank you for coming. The reception will be held at the golf course."

Maya felt tears pile up in her eyes and she sobbed. "I'm going to miss him so much."

Mrs. Dragstedt exhaled. Their eyes met and, for just a second, Maya thought she saw something in hers, a glimpse of sadness behind the cold exterior. But then it was gone.

"Thank you for that. Thank you for coming."

Maya shook Mr. Dragstedt's hand too, then moved on to where her mother stood. She was bawling her eyes out, her makeup running down her cheeks in black stripes.

"Oh, God, Maya, he was so young, you know? Who would do such a horrible thing? I can't believe it."

Her friend Sophia hugged her and held her while Maya's mother cried and blew her nose loudly. Maya looked back at Asgar's parents, who stoically greeted each and every guest and thanked them for coming, like they had just visited for a social event. Why weren't they grieving the way Maya's mother was? Why were they so calm? It made something inside of Maya wrench. She couldn't stop thinking there was something very wrong. What mother didn't cry at her own son's funeral?

They arrived at the golf course for the reception. It was held in the main building with views of the course from the big windows. It was a beautiful landscape all dressed in white. Maya loved the snow. Except for today. Today, it filled Maya with a deep sadness when thinking about the snowball fights she used to have with Asgar.

Samuel came up behind her and put a hand on her shoulder. Maya turned around and smiled when she saw him. Out of the corner of her eye, she saw her mother. She was staring at them, biting her lip between sobs.

Maya and Samuel walked towards the tables with appetizers and started to fill their plates. Maya was starving and started to eat even before she was done loading her plate. A man with a tray asked if she wanted a glass of champagne. She declined with a, *no thank you*, while wondering if it was customary to serve champagne at a funeral.

They found a quiet spot to sit, away from all the people, while they ate. Every now and then, Maya felt overwhelmed by sadness when thinking about Asgar and all the fun they had together and now it happened again.

"I just miss him so terribly," she said.

"He loved you so much," Samuel said.

"And I didn't love him back. I'm an awful human being," Maya said.

"Don't say that."

Maya leaned her head on Samuel's shoulder, then she spotted Leonora Dragstedt entering the building. Maya lifted her head.

"It's her," she said.

"Who?"

"That lady who just entered over there. That's Asgar's sister. I heard my mom and our neighbors talking about her in church."

"That can't be true. Asgar doesn't have a sister."

"Apparently, she ran away with some guy before we were even born. That's what they said, but that's not the strange part."

"What is?"

"It's the same woman from the profile picture. On Facebook. The lady Asgar had written to and asked to meet with."

"Ah, I see," Samuel said. "So, Asgar went behind his parent's back to see his sister, and that probably didn't land well with mommy and daddy dearest."

"You think they killed him because of that?" Maya asked.

"Doesn't really sound like motive enough to me," he said.

"You're right," Maya said and ate a strawberry. "She must have remarried since her name on Facebook was Bergman."

"Or she changed her name because she didn't want

anything to do with her parents or her family anymore," Samuel said.

"Either way, there's bound to be drama once they see her," Maya said, just as Mr. Dragstedt spotted Leonora in the crowd. Maya and Samuel watched as he spoke quietly to Mrs. Dragstedt before they both approached her.

Chapter 32

I COULD BARELY HOLD it together. I hated funerals, but I hated it even more when it was a young kid being buried. I couldn't believe Asgar was gone. I had loved the boy so much and had to admit I had kind of hoped he and Maya would fall in love, especially since they spent so much time together and seemed to care deeply for one another.

But now she was hanging out with her friend Samuel, and the two of them seemed awfully fond of one another in a way I had never seen before with Maya. She had a look in her eyes that I had never seen. All day, I wondered if Samuel was the mysterious night visitor that used the ladder outside her window.

I had to admit they were awfully cute together.

"You want more to eat?" Morten asked as I finished my plate. I looked at him. "Do you even have to ask?"

He laughed, and I got up and went to the buffet, Sophia by my side also ready for a second round. The food was extremely good. Every now and then, I broke down and cried helplessly while eating, thinking about poor Asgar and how he used to come to my house and we would all sit in the kitchen and have coffee and cookies or chocolate and chat.

I looked at the Dragstedts and wondered how they could keep so calm when burying their only son. I don't think I would be able to even stand up if I lost Victor or Maya.

The very thought made me finish my glass of champagne in one drink. Morten was driving me home, so I didn't have to worry about the alcohol. As I put the glass down, I spotted Mr. and Mrs. Dragstedt immersed in a conversation and, seconds later, they were both walking with almost aggressive steps towards the entrance, where I now spotted Leonora Dragstedt.

"Uh-oh," I said and grabbed another glass of champagne from some well-dressed guy with a tray.

"What?" Sophia asked.

"Look. Possible drama coming up."

Sophia looked in the direction of the door and spotted Leonora and the parents now approaching her, their steps determined and faces angry.

"Oh-oh," she said.

They were now talking to her, still keeping their cool. Mr. Dragstedt grabbed Leonora's arm like he wanted to pull her away, but she pulled it free.

"I am sick of this, Dad," she yelled.

Mrs. Dragstedt looked around, corrected her perfect hair with a gentle hand, then smiled at the people around her who had started to stare.

"Leonora, dear," I could hear her say. "Please, just…"

"No," she yelled. "I am sick of this, so sick of the two of you pretendi…" her dad grabbed her arm, forcefully this time, and pulled her away.

"Mom?" she said as he pulled her toward the door.

"You're making a spectacle of yourself, my dear," Mrs.

Dragstedt said. "And of your brother's funeral. I will not have you ruin that too."

Mrs. Dragstedt snorted, corrected her dress, turned on her heel, and smiled as she faced the gaping crowd.

She clapped her hands at the waiters. "Now, if you'll serve the coffee, please. Chop-chop."

Chapter 33

MAYA WATCHED THE SCENE, then grabbed Samuel's hand and pulled him up from his seat.

"Come."

"Where are we going?" he asked as he followed her, running. "Maya? Please, wait up."

She rushed outside, Samuel right behind her. They found Leonora Dragstedt in the parking lot, approaching a car.

"Hurry," Maya said. "She's leaving."

The woman had her hand on the handle of the door and opened it. Maya rushed toward her and reached up a hand to signal for her to wait. She approached her and stopped in front of her, panting.

"Leonora? Leonora Dragstedt?"

The woman paused, then shut the door to the car. She looked at Maya with eyes red from crying.

"It's been awhile since anyone called me that. Can't say it brings back good memories."

"But you are her, right? You're Asgar's sister, right?" Maya asked, panting heavily from running.

The woman sighed. "And who might you be?"

"I...*we* are Asgar's friends," Maya said. "I'm Maya and this is Samuel."

"Okay, Asgar's friends, you have two minutes before this place drives me nuts and I run away screaming. What do you want?"

Maya glanced at Samuel, then back at Leonora. "I... we were just wondering...I mean..."

"Why did Asgar write to you before he died? Why did he ask to meet with you?" Samuel took over.

Leonora bit her lip. "He had recently found out about me. That was why he decided to stay home from the ski trip, that and because he was mad. Who wouldn't be? He wanted to see me, to meet up while they were gone, but I refused to. I couldn't get myself to face my past."

"So, they had never told him about you?" Maya asked.

"What do you think? I was a scandal. They would kill him if they ever found out he saw me."

Leonora realized the unfortunate choice of words, then shook her head. "I mean, not that..."

"Do you think they could?" Maya asked. "Kill him?"

Leonora shook her head. Tears were piling up in her eyes. "I can't...I can't go there again. It was wrong of me to come. No one benefits from me being here. I am sorry. I have to go. It was nice to meet you, Asgar's friends. Thanks for being his friends, while he was still...alive."

Leonora covered her mouth, then rushed into the Volkswagen Beetle. Maya watched as Leonora drove off, tears gushing down her cheeks.

Samuel approached her.

"So, that was Asgar's sister, huh?"

"And the family's best-kept secret, apparently."

"Apparently."

Chapter 34

SHE FOUGHT to open her eyes. Her eyelids were so heavy she could hardly open them up. And, as she finally did, she struggled to see. Spots were dancing in front of Susan's eyes and she felt dizzy even from just lying down.

Between her fingers, she felt the scissors. They were still there. The clocks in front of her showed it was ten o'clock. It was light inside the room; light was coming from beneath the thick velvet curtain. It had to be morning. The man with the mask usually only came to her at night.

She shivered, thinking about him and his scaly skin.

Susan wiggled her fingers and got a better hold on the scissors. She managed to push them open using her two fingers, so she now had the sharp blade to work with. She wiggled it slightly, then managed to get it close to the leather straps around her wrists. It was only the tip of the blade, but by bending her wrist and using her fingers to move it back and forth, she managed to get the blade to rub against the leather. She struggled to push down hard enough on it to make it cut anything.

Susan's wrist hurt like crazy and she groaned in anger

and effort. The other blade was cutting into the palm of her hand as she moved it back and forth and soon she was bleeding. Susan felt dizzy watching the blood, thinking she wasn't certain her body could bear to lose more blood.

Susan moaned in pain but continued, using the one blade as a saw. She had to press harder down on it as the leather started to cave, but that also meant cutting deeper into her own palm, into the wound that was already shaping there. Susan closed her eyes and let out a loud scream as she pressed down hard, then moved it back and forth until, suddenly, the leather strap snapped.

"Ha!" she exclaimed.

Susan moaned in pain but laughed at the same time. She lifted her hand and looked at it, then moved her fingers and wrist freely. She could move her arm all the way up to her elbow, as she was strapped down across her chest and shoulders by another thick leather band.

With the bleeding hand, she moved the scissors to her right hand and cut the strap open, sawing it with the blade, and soon she could move the other hand as well. Next to go down was the strap around her chest, which felt like it took forever to cut through since the leather was so thick, but soon she could move her upper body and sit up, then take care of both her ankles and finally, she was free.

Susan sighed, relieved, and looked down at her body while catching her breath from the effort. She had gotten so skinny. She swung her legs over the edge of the bed and stood up.

She had to hold onto the bed as the dizziness over-whelmed her. She breathed in ragged breaths, closing her eyes as the room spun around her. As she felt it calm down slightly, she opened them again, then looked around and finally dared to let go of the bed and take her first step toward freedom, toward the heavy wooden door in front of her.

As she leaned forward to take the second step, the room spun so fast around her she could no longer stand up.

All she could see was deep darkness.

Chapter 35

THE DRAMA from the reception still lingered with me as we drove into the driveway of our house. Morten was just dropping me and Maya off. He had to go back to the station since they were still on the lookout for Susan Ludvigsen. I was sad because I knew I wasn't going to see him the rest of the day.

"Maybe I'll come by tonight," he said when we kissed goodbye. "If it doesn't get too late."

I sighed as I watched him drive away. I was so tired of living like this. Why couldn't we just move in together? Then we would at least see each other every day when we woke up and went to bed. The way it was now, we had to schedule seeing each other, and that was hard with his line of work. Sometimes, he would stop by for lunch during his shift, but that was just for half an hour. I missed him so much when we weren't together.

I thought about the Dragstedts and that woman who was Asgar's sister. Maya had told me in the car that Asgar hadn't even known he had a sister. What kind of people would shut out their own daughter out and keep a boy from knowing his sister? It made no sense to me.

"So, you and Samuel, huh?" I tried, while we walked up the steps to the house. I had been trying to get courage enough to ask her about him all the way back but hadn't gotten it until now. I wanted to ask, but at the same time, I knew Maya was very private about her life and I didn't want to pry. Well… that's not entirely true. I wanted to pry, of course, I did. I just didn't want her to be angry with me for doing so.

She gave me a look. "We're just friends," she said, yet blushing lightly. "That's all."

"Really?" I asked, thinking about the ladder still leaning up against the side of the house.

She turned around and looked straight into my eyes. "Really."

I sensed I needed to back off, so, of course, I didn't.

"Just be safe, okay?" I mumbled.

"MOM!"

Maya stared at me, eyes wide and arms held out in front of her. I think she might have seriously thought about killing me in that instant. I could be wrong, but it was that kind of look she gave me. "That's the most cringy thing you have ever said to me, ugh."

I smiled. "Maya, you'll be turning eighteen soon. I can't keep an eye on you forever. We never talked about these things and I…"

She pointed at me, her finger vibrating with anger. "I am not doing this with you. I am not."

"Okay, okay," I said, resigned. "I just know that it happened to me at your age. Just sayin'."

"Argh! Mom, you're so embarrassing. Are you even listening to yourself? Ugh. I can't deal with you right now," she said, then stormed up to the door and ran inside.

I walked in after her, but she was already gone, probably already in her room, texting all her friends about how embarrassing her mother was. I took off my coat and boots, then walked into the living room where my parents were sitting, my mom in my dad's lap, making out.

I cringed. "Yak," I mumbled and left them, then went into the kitchen to get a cup of coffee.

In there, I found Victor and Skye. They were sitting at the table in the middle of what seemed to be a deep conversation that apparently required no spoken words. In front of Victor's face floated a spoon.

"What are you doing?" I almost screamed.

The spoon fell to the table. Victor looked at me. He smiled. "She taught me. Skye taught me how to do that."

I felt a twitch in my right eye as I stared at my son, who once again lifted the spoon into the air, apparently by using nothing but the power of his mind.

"This is a madhouse," I mumbled under my breath. "Coffee. I need coffee. I need coffee now."

Chapter 36

GIOVANNI DIDN'T WANT to be a waiter. Giovanni was a musician. He played the guitar and sang. It was all he wanted to do with his life, and so many times he had tried to explain it to his dad. But his dad wouldn't hear of it. Giovanni was supposed to take over the restaurant after his dad, so he could retire in a few years. That was the plan, and there was nothing he could say to change it.

The family had moved to Denmark and Fanoe Island back in the seventies and his dad had at first tried his luck as a musician himself, but since it didn't bring money enough to support his family, he got the idea to open up an Italian restaurant, the first on the island. And what a success it turned out to be.

At first, the islanders were quite reluctant to try something new, but once they did, they couldn't get enough of Alessandro's pasta dishes. Even though he tried to explain to the Danes that pasta was a first course, *a primo piatto*, they wouldn't listen and kept ordering it as an entree, as their only meal, and soon, he changed his menu to please the customers. Today, he was known widely for his pasta dishes and people would come to the island just to taste his delicacies.

Giovanni knew his dad was proud of his restaurant and so was he, as his son. But he wasn't very interested in taking over the restaurant one day and especially not in working there for his dad as a waiter. Giovanni believed he was wasting his time, time he should be spending writing songs and creating music. He should be playing in front of a crowd in clubs and bars, building an audience. Just playing on street corners—even if it was quite difficult in a cold country like Denmark—would be better than this.

Giovanni sighed and took the order from a couple who had just arrived at the restaurant. He smiled and made sure they were happy and well taken care of. Giovanni's dad wanted him to know the business from the inside, that was why he had hired him as first a busboy, then a waiter. He had to work his way up like the rest of them. Now, Giovanni couldn't cook. So, the kitchen wasn't an option, but his dad didn't cook anymore either. Those days were over. Now, he had cooks working for him, using his traditional Italian recipes that he brought with him from his grandmother, who got them from her grandmother.

As soon as Alessandro retired, Giovanni would be the sole owner of those recipes and responsible for passing on the family traditions.

But Giovanni hated pasta, he hated marinara sauce and the smell of the kitchen. He loathed having to deal with customers more than anything. It simply wasn't him.

Giovanni walked to the back and gave them the order in the kitchen, then spotted his guitar. It was leaning up against the wall, still in its bag. He looked at his watch. It was almost time for his break.

He grabbed the guitar and snuck outside to the back, behind the restaurant, and sat with his back leaned up against the dumpster, then strummed his guitar, closing his eyes and imagining standing on a stage in front of thousands of people playing them his own songs. He parted his lips and started to sing, to let out the words of his favorite song that he wrote to the love of his life. Her name was Lotte and they met in high school. It was a long time ago now, at least that was how it felt, but he still remembered her smell, the sound of her voice, and her laughter.

Giovanni closed his eyes and sang for her once again, listening to the sound of his own voice bouncing off the walls of the surrounding buildings. It sounded good and made him feel so good about himself. He sighed and opened his eyes when he heard something. It sounded like low, weak knocking. Giovanni turned his head and looked at the dumpster behind him, then shook his head.

No, it couldn't have come from there. It was impossible.

He sat back down, closed his eyes, and was about to sing more when he heard it again, this time louder. Giovanni shrieked.

"W-who's there?"

Another knock. This time, there was no doubt in Giovanni's mind where it came from.

Heart in his throat, Giovanni crawled up into the dumpster and started to dig, throwing bags of leftover food into the street. When he stopped and saw what had made the sound, he realized he would never be able to sing again.

Chapter 37

"HE DID WHAT? You're kidding me, right?"

Sophia stared at me in disbelief. I shook my head. I was cleaning up after dinner that I had made for the entire family. Sophia came over for a glass of wine while her mother hung out with her kids.

"I'm afraid not. The kid did it and it doesn't end there. At dinner, he kept moving his utensils that same way, and I had to stop him so my mom and dad wouldn't see it. I don't want them to think he's weirder than they already do. Besides, I don't know how to deal with it right now with everything else that is going on."

"I…I've heard about people who could do stuff like that," she said. "I've read about it, but…wow. I wasn't sure I actually believed it was possible before. I think I need to see it with my own eyes."

"I am not getting my son to show you," I said and wiped the last pot dry and put it away. "See. That's exactly what I'm afraid of. That he'll end up like some circus freak. I ain't doing it."

Sophia nodded. "All right, all right, calm down. I was

just curious. I think you're right about being careful about this. Who knows what he might be used for if he ends up in the wrong hands?"

I closed the cabinet. "The thing is, I don't know how to help him control it. I don't want him to be embarrassed about it; I want him to use it, to master it. I think it is awesome what he can do, I truly do, but I need him to understand that he needs to keep it to himself. I don't know how to make him understand that."

Sophia nodded, then sipped her wine. "Wow. It's never boring around here, is it?"

"I'm telling you," I said with a sigh. "It's a madhouse lately. Between Victor and his creepy new friend and Maya having boys up in her room, I am about to lose it completely."

"Maya has boys in her room?"

"Well…boy. You know Samuel, right?"

"Sure do. Handsome devil and sweet too. She could do a lot worse than him, I think."

"Me too. I just don't know how to talk to her about it. She gets all angry and starts to yell and says I am cringy and stuff like that."

"I'll have a chat with her for you if you like."

"You'd do that?"

"Of course."

"I just need to make sure that she is staying…safe."

Sophia winked. "I am the woman for that. If anyone can scare her away from having sex—or at least unprotected sex—it's the woman with six kids. If the talk won't work, then I'll let her babysit all of them at once. She'll never even think about having sex again. Ever."

I laughed and sat down with my glass in hand. I lifted it and clanged it against hers.

"To no sex."

"To no sex."

I chuckled after drinking, then looked at my phone. It was vibrating on the counter. I grabbed it. It was Morten.

"I am sorry. I can't make it tonight. Someone just found a body in a dumpster downtown."

I exhaled. "Is it Susan Ludvigsen? Please, tell me it isn't her?"

"We don't know yet. I'm on my way there now. Apparently, she is still alive, the paramedics said, but only barely holding on."

"Wow. Guess I'll hope to see you tomorrow then?" I said.

"Let's try for that. I have to go, we're there now."

"Bye."

I hung up and lifted my glass again with a sigh.

"Guess the no sex part goes for me as well."

Chapter 38

MAYA WAS SITTING at the computer when she heard the rubble hit her window. She got up and opened it, then peeked down. There he was, looking more handsome than ever.

He crawled up the ladder and Maya just prayed her mother wouldn't hear him or accidentally see him. After the little "chat" they almost had today outside the house, she was terrified that her mom would think she was sneaking him in to have sex. It was the last thing on Maya's mind. She had kissed him twice and that was as far as she dared to go.

"Hi," he said as he peeked inside. He smiled, his pearly white teeth shining almost unnaturally in the darkness.

"Come on in," she said, rushing him. "Get inside before we both freeze to death."

She closed the window, then turned. They suddenly stood face to face. She let out a small gasp. He grabbed her face between his hands, then kissed her. Maya let him, feeling the warmth of the kiss spread throughout her body. She closed her eyes and enjoyed the kiss.

When she opened them, she looked into his eyes, feeling herself getting totally sucked into them. Then she pulled away, shyly.

"I take it that wasn't why you asked me to come?" he asked.

Maya shook her head. "But it was nice," she said, blushing.

He smirked. "I kind of liked it too."

She sighed, then shook her head. "I texted for you to come because I found something," she said, getting back on track, shaking the tingling feeling in her stomach that the kiss had left her with.

Samuel lit up. "You did?"

Maya nodded, biting her lip. She went to the laptop and turned the screen, so he could better see.

"I went through some of his files and found this."

Samuel approached the screen and looked at it. Maya felt her heart race when looking at him, but tried to push it back in her mind. She forced herself to not think about him in that way, to prevent herself from blushing constantly when he looked at her. She didn't want to come off as desperate or too eager.

"What the heck…?

"I know," she said.

"I…I don't believe this? Is this really true?"

She shrugged. "Well, it's there. In writing."

Samuel ran a hand through his thick blond hair "Wow. I am shocked," he said, still looking at the screen.

"Guess I was wrong when I said the sister was this family's best-kept secret," she said.

"You sure were," Samuel said and sat down. He scrolled down then back up again and kept reading the same line in the document. He turned his head and looked at Maya, his eyes shocked.

"This is."
"And it provides a motive," Maya said.

Chapter 39

IT WAS nighttime when she woke up. Susan had a terrible headache and felt so weak she could hardly sit up. The room was spinning, the clocks ticking loudly, making her headache even worse.

But it wasn't midnight yet.

"I can still make it out," she mumbled, her tongue so dry, it stuck to the roof of her mouth. "Before he gets here."

Susan got up on her knees, reached out her hand, and grabbed the bed, then pulled herself up using all her strength. She realized she was stronger now than she had been earlier. That was probably why he always came at this time of night because this was when she had the most blood in her.

Or maybe he's a vampire who only wakes up at midnight. To feast on your blood.

She shivered at the thought, then bent forward to try and make the room stop spinning. It helped. She had seen him drink her blood. After tapping it into small bags, he would attach the tube from the bags to the ones sticking out of his mask and suck it into his mouth, like he was drinking from a darn straw. She had heard him slurp and swallow loudly as he gulped it down. It had freaked her out completely.

"I gotta get out of here," she mumbled and stood up straight, then waited a few seconds to get the room to stop spinning. "Before he comes."

She fought to keep standing, then took one step toward the door, then another, and soon she was walking, moving toward it. Panting, she grabbed the handle and leaned on the door for a few seconds to make sure she wouldn't faint again. This was her last chance to ever get out of here alive.

Susan grabbed the handle and moved it down, then opened the door and revealed a hallway. It had marble floors and antiques everywhere. Mostly clocks. A large grandfather clock reached almost to the ceiling, a carriage clock with a handle on top was on a tabletop. There was an octagonal schoolhouse clock in a pendulum box mounted on the wall, a mantel clock in a drum-shaped case, a dresser with a desk clock and clocks on the walls, hundreds of radio-controlled clocks, showing the time all over the world.

Susan felt sick when staring at the many clocks and especially when listening to them as she hurried down the hallway, feeling like the clocks were rotating and almost whirling around her, constantly reminding her that she had to *hurry, hurry, hurry*.

She spotted what looked like a front door at the end of the hallway, then hurried towards it the best she could without fainting. She fought to push through the over-whelming sensation, the tickling and prickling in her fingertips and her arms from the lack of blood in those areas, the dizziness and the lack of strength. Susan almost cried with determination, seeing the door come closer and closer. The big hand-carved wooden door approached slowly while the sound of the ticking clocks buzzed in her ears.

She had almost made it there and believed she could feel the coldness of the handle in her hand when she heard a sound that made her stop instantly.

The sound of someone moaning.

Susan tried to block out the sound, but she couldn't. Just as she was about to grab the door handle, she turned instead and went to another door, then opened it, pushing it open with the last of her strength.

What she saw in there instantly made fall to her knees and cry.

Chapter 40

MY SLEEP WAS UNEASY. Maybe it was the wine, maybe the chocolate I ate just before bedtime, I don't know. But I couldn't find rest. Maybe it was because I couldn't stop thinking about what Morten had told me, that they had found someone in a dumpster downtown. He had called before I went to bed and told me the guy was barely alive and that he was almost empty of blood. They had taken him to the hospital on the mainland, transporting him on the ferry, and he was now fighting for his life. Morten and his team had asked the nurses to make sure to notify him when he woke up—if he woke up—and then they had come back to start the search for Susan Ludvigsen all over again. They were realizing that it was more vital than ever that they find her, and they feared the worst.

The boy they had found was also a senior at the high school, or he used to be, but was expelled about a month ago and had run away from home because he was afraid of what his parents would do when they found out he was expelled from school. Everyone, including his parents, thought he had left the island like most kids who ran away did.

That was probably what was keeping me up all night. Was someone targeting the teenagers at the high school for some reason? Was some sicko kidnapping the high school kids and emptying them of their blood?

Why?

The good part was that Vincent, the boy found in the dumpster, was still alive and maybe he would be able to tell us more, when or *if* he woke up. Morten had told me he thought the killer probably believed Vincent was dead and tried to get rid of him, not knowing he was still alive, clinging to life.

I sat up in bed, my heart pounding while thinking about Maya. I wasn't so sure it was safe for her to go to school anymore, but she could hardly stay home for weeks or possibly even months before they caught this creep. I could hardly go with her and keep my eyes on her constantly either. She was, after all, seventeen years old.

I was staring at the window in the darkness and all the light coming from the street when I decided to go to the bathroom. That would probably make it easier to sleep.

I walked into the hallway and found the door to the bathroom slightly open. I pushed it all the way open and stepped inside only to find Skye in there, standing on the tiles, staring at the toilet bowl.

"Skye?" I asked. "Are you okay?"

Her little body was shaking. She didn't turn her head to look at me. She stood like she was frozen and stared at the toilet. I walked closer and looked down into it, then realized the water inside of it was moving, splashing up against the sides.

"What's wrong?" I asked again, even though I knew she wouldn't answer. I looked into her eyes and saw the terror in them. I tried to calm her down and gave her a reassuring smile. "It does that sometimes. I think it's the old plumbing."

The girl stared at me, her eyes big and wide, her slim shoulders trembling.

"You hear it too, huh?" I said with a sigh.

Victor had been hearing things for a long time now, he had told me. It came from the sewer, he said, and it was everywhere on the island or under it, as he said. I had told him a million times it was just because the plumbing under the island, the pipes and sewers, were so old they would often make loud noises, especially when it was cold outside, but he didn't believe me.

"Yeah, Victor is scared of it too," I said. "I often think he hears things more vividly than the rest of us. He does tend to hear things I don't, and he gets annoyed with loud noises. Sometimes, I can't even get him to go to the bathroom. He would rather keep it in till he's about to burst than face this fear of his. Guess you're just like him, huh?"

I grabbed her hand in mine.

"It's okay," I said. "It's just an old house on an old island with old sewers. Nothing to be scared of. Come, let me get you back to bed."

Chapter 41

"TIM?"

Susan stared at the boy in the bed. She could hardly recognize him. It was like he had completely withered away. Yet she recognized the terror-stricken eyes looking back at her.

She was crying and couldn't hold it back. She didn't know Tim very well, but she knew who he was and had spoken to him several times. He had been in the other class at the high school. He had moved away before Christmas and was supposed to be in Germany with his parents, where his dad was starting a new job.

Susan approached Tim, looking at his tiny body beneath her. He was strapped down the same way she had been, with a thick leather strap around his shoulders and chest and hands and legs strapped to the bed. Not that it was necessary to keep him tied up anymore. There was no way he could go anywhere. He kept falling in and out of consciousness and was barely breathing. Susan touched his pale skin gently, then spoke to him.

"I'm gonna get us out of here. I'll run and get help."

She sobbed while realizing Tim might not even have that much time, that leaving him might be the same as killing him. She reached over to grab the straps, opening them, when she heard the sound of more moaning coming from behind another door. She rushed to it and opened it.

Then her heart stopped.

In there, she saw four more teenagers in dog cages. All were skinny and pale and looked more dead than alive. Susan gasped and clasped her mouth. Susan knew these four kids, but they weren't from her school. They lived in Sonderho, a town at the other end of the island, and they were school dropouts. Some came from foster homes, others had parents so drunk they didn't even care what their kids were up to. They were troubled kids.

The kind of kids no one would miss.

Susan fell to her knees, staring at their almost lifeless bodies, then felt the terror strike her as she realized these kids had been here for a long time, probably a lot longer than her. These kids were dying, yet he was keeping them here, why? To squeeze out a few last drops of blood from them?

The thought made her sick to her stomach.

Susan grabbed the door to one of the cages, but it was locked. She pulled it in frustration, crying in desperation, then fell back on her knees, exhausted, while the boy behind the bars was barely breathing. She wondered if he even knew what was going on anymore or if he had given up and sunk into the blissful darkness. Had he embarked on his path to leave this earth?

"I'll get help," she whispered to him and to the rest of them, who barely noticed she was there.

"I promise you. I'll get help."

She pulled herself up to her feet, stood for a few seconds and gathered all the strength she could when she heard all the clocks in the house simultaneously strike. They were chiming, bonging and bursting into a variety of tunes, almost like a concert.

It was midnight.

Chapter 42

SHE HID in a cabinet and closed the door by keeping her fingers in the crack, holding the door closed. She heard the front door open.

A cold rush of air went through the house and then everything went quiet. Susan held her breath as she looked out of the crack in the cabinet door. In the distance, she saw the man, the shadowy figure as he rushed across the marble tiles, making no sound as he moved, and she wondered if his feet even touched the floor. He was wearing his mask, as usual, probably ready to enter her room and start the tapping of her blood. He disappeared, then came back into the hallway with all the clocks. It didn't take him long before he noticed the open doors leading to Tim and then to the room with the other teenagers.

Susan tried hard not to make a sound, but her fingers were hurting from holding the door closed.

"Susan?" he called, breathing heavily behind the mask. "Where are you? You know you can't hide from me. Su-u-san. Su-u-san. SU-SAN!"

He looked at the teenagers, then rustled one of the cages.

"Where is she?"

The boy inside of it didn't react. The man calmed himself down. She noticed that his skin wasn't as scaly when he entered the room but now it seemed to be cracking and he looked at his hands, lifting them up in the air.

"I need her, damn it," he said. "'Look at what is happening to me. You're doing this to me, Susan. You hear me? You're the reason I am falling apart now. Please, just show yourself. I need you. I need your blood. All the others, they are almost empty now, whereas you still have the good stuff inside of you, the stuff I need. Yours is the best, Susan, did you know that? Yours is the best, better than any of the others."

Susan held onto the cabinet door, her fingertips painfully strained. She could see him moving around the room in his black clothes, rushing past her soundlessly.

Susan held her breath as he started to open the built-in cabinets one after another, starting at the end of the room and moving up toward her. It was only a matter of seconds before he would open hers.

Susan closed her eyes as she heard the doors slam against the wall behind them, then decided to make a run for it before he reached hers. She jumped out and fell onto the tiles.

"There you are," the man said and rushed toward her, his feet barely touching the ground. Susan jolted to her feet and started to run when a hand grabbed her by the throat and made her fall back.

"There you are," he repeated, holding her tightly. He smelled her skin. "You seem to be bursting with the good stuff. Oh, how I crave your blood right now, so badly I could almost…"

He pulled her toward the door, but Susan screamed and fought him the best she could. She bit him, hard, sinking her teeth into his old and scaly skin; then, as he roared in pain and removed his hand, she hit her clenched fist into his mask. The blow was forceful and made him pull back, while her hand was hurting from the meeting with the thick plastic. To her surprise, the mask had hurt the man's face pretty badly because he was screaming in pain and, as he did, Susan turned around, rushed back into the hallway, and sprang for the front door.

Chapter 43

SHE WAS SITTING in the terminal, drinking coffee, waiting for the ferry to arrive, when they approached her. Maya felt nervous, yet very determined as she, along with Samuel, walked up to Leonora Dragstedt. The woman glared at them with great surprise.

"Not you again."

"Yes, us," Maya said as she pulled out a chair and sat down.

Leonora looked at her watch. "I should be getting back to my car soon. I have to be in it when they start to board the ferry."

Maya pulled out a piece of paper and placed it on the table in front of her. "We need to talk."

Leonora looked at it, then sunk back in her chair. "W-where did you get this?"

"Your brother's computer," Samuel said.

"But he isn't really your brother," Maya said.

Leonora stared at Asgar's birth certificate in front of her, where her name was written on top. She shook her head with a sigh.

"He's your son?" Maya asked.

She nodded.

"And you never told him?" Samuel asked.

"How could you keep that a secret from him?" Maya asked.

"I had no choice. I was young," she said. "About your age. I got pregnant. It was a scandal; my parents wouldn't have it and they sent me away. They paid off Sven, the father of the child, and sent both of us away. Sven spent all the money on gambling and, last I heard, he's back on the island, working at the harbor. But he kept his promise to my parents and never told a soul. Meanwhile, I stayed at my aunt's house north of Copenhagen till it was time for me to give birth. As soon as I came home from the hospital, I found my parents waiting at my aunt's house. They took him. They told me to never come back to the island again. I lived with my aunt for a few months before she told me I had to leave. I found a place to live with the sister of a friend I knew till I could graduate high school, then got a job and worked my way through college. I did my best to forget my past and especially the child. I even got married, but we couldn't have any more children. I tried to move on and never look back, I really did."

"But he found you?" Maya asked.

She nodded, a tear shaping in the corner of her eye. "One day, he wrote to me on Facebook. He had searched for me, he said, and now he wanted to meet. I didn't know if he knew or not, but now that you found the birth certificate, I'm guessing he did. He must have found it among my parents' belongings."

"He wanted to meet you because you were his mother," Samuel said. "But you refused to."

"What could I have done?" Leonora asked. "I wanted

to meet with him, I wanted to so badly to see my only child, but I didn't dare to. What if my parents found out?"

"You were afraid of them?"

"Not for me. I am a grown woman, but for him. He was in their care. I was scared of what they might do to him if he found out."

Maya sighed and nodded. "And now you worry that something did happen, right?"

She nodded, the tear escaping her eye and rolling across her cheek. "I fear he might have confronted them with it, asking them about it, telling them he wanted to meet me, and then they…"

"Killed him," Samuel said.

Leonora sniffled and looked up, then nodded. "Yes."

Chapter 44

I WAS SITTING in my kitchen writing on my laptop when a car drove up in front of my house. I had let Victor stay home from school one more day to spend it with Skye. They were playing in the living room, so I hurried up and closed the door before I walked to the front door and opened it. I grabbed my coat and put it on.

Out of the car stepped Maya, Samuel, and Leonora Dragstedt. It was an odd combination, but with what was going on these days, I was getting quite used to odd.

"Maya? What's going on?" I asked.

She approached me. The wind bit my cheeks.

"We need your help, Mom. We need to talk to Morten."

"Morten? But why?"

Maya sighed.

"What's going on, Maya? You're scaring me."

"We know who killed Asgar," she said.

I stared at my daughter, eyebrows lifted. "Really?"

Leonora stepped forward, waving and smiling awkwardly. "Hi. I'm Leonora," she said.

"Nice to meet you," I said, shaking her hand, then rubbing my arms because I was freezing. I was hesitant to let them all inside since I was scared they might see Victor and Skye engaged in one of their games of making things float and throwing them around. "Could someone please explain what is going on?"

"Leonora is…was Asgar's mother," Maya said. "She was pregnant when her parents sent her away then took the baby and raised Asgar as their own to avoid a scandal. We believe Asgar found out and confronted them and then they…killed him."

"Really?" I asked.

Maya nodded. "We talked Leonora into telling her part of the story, but we don't want it to be to those people from Copenhagen. We trust Morten, so we wanted to tell him everything first."

I nodded. "I can't blame you, but Maya, there's…"

"I tried to call him," Maya said, cutting me off, "but he isn't answering. Do you know where he is?"

"He's at the golf club. They have the grand opening of the new hole today. Hole thirteen got a makeover as far as I heard. Maybe got a new sand trap or something, I don't know. Everyone is down there, the mayor, the commissioners, and everyone who is anybody on the island is present."

Maya nodded. "We'll find him there then."

"Wait," I said. "I'll go with you. Let me just call Sophia. She can stay with Victor and Skye."

"Mom, Victor is twelve years old, he can stay at home alone for a little while. He'll be fine."

I sighed, phone in my hand, dialing Sophia's number. "Not your brother, Maya. Not Victor."

Chapter 45

MAYOR RASMUSSEN WAS in the middle of her speech when we entered the clubhouse. It was packed with people from all over the island, all dressed nicely for the occasion. The opening of a new hole on the golf course was a big event around here, or at least they managed to make us all think it was. The local newspaper, the *Fanoe Gazette* was even there, and so was the local TV station, TV-Fanoe. They all turned their heads as we entered.

The mayor continued her speech, looking every bit as mad as she had always been.

"As always, I would like to thank my family for supporting me," she said like she was in the middle of a thank you speech for winning an award. As usual, she had probably completely forgotten why she was really there. But people thought it was a good speech and clapped. I spotted Morten in his uniform standing by the end wall and approached him.

"Emma?" he whispered. "What are you doing here? I'm working, you do know that, right?"

"Yes. That's why I'm here."

"Maya? Samuel? What are you all doing here? And Leonora Dragstedt? Why is she here?"

I showed him the birth certificate. He read it, then looked up at me. "What on earth is this? What's going on?"

"We think Asgar's parents killed him," I said, a little too quietly to be heard over the clapping, when suddenly the clapping stopped, and all eyes were on us. Even the mayor was staring.

I smiled awkwardly. "Because of this," I continued.

"What's going on here?" Mrs. Dragstedt asked and elbowed her way through the crowd. "Emma Frost? What on earth are you doing here? This is an invite-only event, not open to the public. Oh, maybe you're working on one of your delightful books? I hardly think this place is cliché-filled enough for you. You'll have more fun down at the harbor with your little friends."

Mrs. Dragstedt laughed. I looked her in the eye, then showed her the birth certificate.

Her smile froze.

"Care to elaborate?" I asked. "Maybe in front of your guests?"

"Oh, please," she said.

Her daughter stepped forward. "I told them every-thing, Mom."

Mrs. Dragstedt stared at her, contempt in her eyes. "You would, wouldn't you? You love to stir the pot a little. Cause a little havoc because that's what you love, isn't it? You love to see your mother in pain, don't you?"

"You're the one who has inflicted an entire life of pain on me."

"Oh, please, because I saved you from embarrassment? At least you had a life. You could move on and forget. I was the one who had to live with the shame each and every day of my life. Every day. Every time I…looked at him, at my own son."

Leonora was crying now, holding a hand to her chest. "He was mine, Mom. He was my son and you…you took him from me. Now you have taken him away forever."

My eyes met Morten's and he understood. He walked up to Mrs. Dragstedt. Her husband came up behind her.

"Mr. and Mrs. Dragstedt. I need you to come to the station with me. I think we need to have a talk."

Part IV

TWO DAYS LATER

Chapter 46

I WAS WALKING the dogs at night, as usual, trying hard to keep warm. My breath froze in front of me as I yelled at Kenneth, who had run astray—also as usual.

"Kenneth! I want to go home. Where are you?"

I walked up into the dunes and looked for him, using my flashlight to follow his tracks, when suddenly I saw another set of tracks, what looked like footprints in the snow, but not ordinary footprints, these were made by a set of bare feet.

"Who walks around without shoes in this cold?" I mumbled to Brutus, who was right behind me, not making a sound.

I followed the tracks and my flashlight fell on more tracks. I continued following them and soon they took me to a small desolate summer cabin between tall trees. I gasped, remembering the cabin from the other day when we had searched for Susan. There had been a man inside of it, a creepy old man who hadn't had any lights turned on. He had freaked me out a little bit.

Was he the one walking around barefoot?

I followed the footprints up to the front door, where I also found Kenneth. He was sitting nicely in front of the door, staring at it, not making a sound, which was very unusual for him. Brutus, on the other hand, approached the door, sat next to Kenneth, then gave one large deep bark, like when he had seen Skye in the tree.

"Is someone in there?" I asked and looked at the tracks leading up to the door.

I walked to the window and looked inside, shining my flashlight into the living room of the old cabin. My light fell on a small body inside of it, lying on the floor, eyes closed, paler than my bed sheets. Her arms were above her head, her palms open, one of them showing a deep wound.

"Susan," I exclaimed.

Oh, dear God. Oh, dear God, no.

I rushed to the front door and found it unlocked, then pushed it open. I hurried inside and knelt next to her, feeling her throat for a pulse. It was there, but it was very, very slow.

"She's freezing," I said to the two dogs. "We need to get her warmed up, fast. We can't wait for Dr. Williamsen to get here."

Dr. Williamsen was the island's only doctor and, even though he had an ambulance that his wife drove, they would still have to take her to the mainland to get her to the hospital.

I grabbed her tiny body in my arms and carried her out of the house, the dogs walking by my side. It felt like they knew this was serious, this was no time to run off or bark or act out.

I held Susan's body close to mine and hurried across the beach, my feet struggling to run in the snow, but the closer I got to the ocean, the thinner the snow became.

The ocean had started to freeze, and big blocks of ice were pushed onshore. I ran the best I could, holding Susan close, till I reached my own house. I put her down in my living room, next to the burning fireplace, and covered her in blankets.

Then I grabbed my phone; first, I called Dr. Williamsen, then Morten.

Chapter 47

"SHE SUFFERED A MASSIVE BLOOD LOSS."

Dr. Williamsen looked at me from behind his thick glasses. I had known him for many years now but never seen him this serious. "I don't know if she can survive it," he said. "Problem is, they have suspended the ferry for the next twenty-four hours because of the ice. They're waiting for the ice breakers to come and clear the way, but they're busy all over the country."

I stared at him, then at Morten next to me. "But... surely there is something else they can do to get her to a hospital?" I asked.

Dr. Williamsen sighed. "Not right now, no."

"What about a helicopter? Can't they pick her up in a helicopter and take her there?"

He shook his head. "The only medical helicopter we have is in Copenhagen and it's in use because of a rescue mission on Oresund, where a ship has collided with the bridge. There are many who are severely injured."

"So, that's just it?" I asked. "She's stuck here? The girl is half dead, how...how am I supposed...?"

"Emma," Morten said. "We are all doing the best we can."

"I am terribly sorry," Dr. Williamsen said.

I nodded. "I know. I know." I glanced at Susan lying on the couch by the fireplace. She was still so pale it was creepy. Maya was standing in the doorway of the living room, staring at her, terror on her face.

I walked to Maya and grabbed her in my arms. "It's going to be okay," I said. "We'll take care of her."

"I have hooked her up with a saltwater drip," Dr. Williamsen said. "And I had a couple of bags of blood for her that my wife will make sure get inside of her. I have more at the clinic that I can bring in the morning, but this should do for now. If you can get her to drink something, preferably a Coke or something with sugar in it, that would be awesome. And you're sure it's okay for her to stay here?" he asked. "We could take her to my clinic, but I think she would be better off here. To be honest, her chances are better if we don't move her."

I nodded, feeling slightly woozy at the thought of having this kind of responsibility.

"Sure. She can stay as long as needed."

Dr. Williamsen put a hand on my shoulder. "You're an angel, Emma. We'll, of course, stay here for tonight to keep an eye on her progress."

"I've tried to reach her mother, but no one seems to be able to find her," Morten said with a sigh. "Not even down behind Netto or in that shed by the harbor where she usually hangs out. My guess is she's on a bender somewhere. I've asked Allan and the boys to go search for her in the usual places."

"Until then, we'll be here for you, Susan," I said and grabbed her hand in mine. I rubbed it the way Dr. Williamsen had told me was good for her circulation. To sort of massage the blood around, *to get it pumping*, as he put it.

The poor girl was hooked up to all kinds of instruments, monitoring her heart rate, her pulse, her blood levels, and so on. And my living room had turned into a hospital. Maya came closer and sat down on the couch across from Susan.

"W-will she survive, Mom?" she asked.

I shrugged, then sat next to her, holding her hand in mine. "I have to be honest and say that I don't know." I forced a smile. "But we're allowed to hope, right?"

She nodded. "How did this happen to her? I don't understand."

"I know, sweetie. Me either."

"Do you think she was taken by the same person who killed Asgar?" she asked.

"I have a feeling it might be the same person, yes."

"But...I don't get it. I thought it was his parents? I thought..."

I pulled her close to me and put her head on my shoulder. "I know, sweetie. I know you do. They have been the main suspects for some time now, and they did have that motive, but...well, no one has been able to prove their guilt so far, and they keep claiming they're innocent. They have good alibies at the ski resort. Plus, there was also Vincent. And now Susan. I think this might be a little bigger than what we initially thought."

I thought about Vincent, the boy found in a dumpster downtown. He was still in the hospital in Esbjerg, on the mainland. No one knew what happened to him, how he ended up in the dumpster, drained of blood. He still hadn't woken up and they worried he never would. I looked at Susan while thinking about him, wondering if any of them

would ever be able to tell who had hurt them like that,
what kind of beast had done this to them.

Chapter 48

SUSAN WAS MAKING progress already the next morning, Dr. Williamsen told me. I slept on the other couch after tucking Maya in and reassuring her everything was going to be just fine. My neck was hurting when I woke up and I needed lots of coffee to get through the day. I made breakfast for everyone and we all ate in my kitchen. I had told Maya she could skip school today and sleep in, while Victor and Skye were eating with us, engaged in a conversation no one could hear.

"She still has a long way to go," Dr. Williamsen said, slurping his coffee, jam from his toast stuck in his beard. "But so far, she is doing really well."

He took another bite and his wife next to him nodded. I smiled and served them some more coffee. "That's good news, then?" I said.

Dr. Williamsen nodded. "I'll see if I can get it arranged for her to be transported to the hospital today."

"Sounds good," I said, not quite listening anymore. My eyes were on Victor, who had his glass floating in the air in front of him, a blissful smile on his face. I rushed to him, grabbed the glass, and put it down, chuckling awkwardly. "Victor is into magic these days," I said.

"Ah, how nice," Dr. Williamsen chuckled. "I used to be quite the magician myself in my younger years."

"Could you do this?" Victor asked. Before I could react, his fork lifted itself from the tabletop and stood up straight.

Dr. Williamsen stared at it, baffled. "No. I must say, I have never done anything like that before. You're good, son. What are you using? Strings?"

I grabbed the fork and put it back down. Victor looked at Skye. He said something to her, I am sure he did, because she smiled too, then made all her long blonde hair stand up on her head.

"Oh, my," Mrs. Williamsen said.

The kids laughed.

"Maybe you should take your friend outside and play for a little while," I said to Victor.

The hair came down, and the two of them made plans I obviously knew nothing about, then got up and rushed out of the kitchen.

"Kids today," Mrs. Williamsen said, shaking her head.

"Who is the girl?" Dr. Williamsen asked. "I don't think I've seen her before. I usually know all the kids around here, you know since I am the only doctor here."

"She's just visiting," I said as I grabbed the coffee pot and swung it. "Refills, anyone?"

They both smiled.

"Oh, yes, thank you," Dr. Williamsen said and held out his cup. "I could certainly use some more."

"Only half a cup for me," Mrs. Williamsen said.

I poured them some more when my phone started to ring, and I picked it up. It was HP from Fishy Pines.

"We haven't seen Victor in quite some time. Is everything all right?"

"Ah, yes. He's not been feeling too well. He'll be back soon."

"Oh, so he is better. Maybe we'll see him tomorrow then?"

I smiled. "Yes. As a matter of fact, I was planning on taking him tomorrow."

"Great. Maybe we can have a little chat then."

"Sure."

I hung up feeling like a kid who had skipped school without my parents knowing.

Dr. Williamsen looked at me. "Victor hasn't been well?"

I forced a smile. "He's fine. He's just been wanting to spend time with his new friend while she's here. That's all."

"Ah, I see. I didn't quite understand it, he seemed so fine just then. As a matter of fact, he seemed better than I have ever seen him."

I sighed. "I know. She's been good for him. She's been really good."

Chapter 49

MAYA WAS RESTLESS ALL DAY. She couldn't stand the thought of having Susan down in her living room, dry as a bone, just lying there, waiting for what? To die?

It made her miserable. Especially when knowing this had to be what Asgar had gone through right before he died. This same slow sneaky death where you simply withered away.

The worst part was that Maya had thought she had found the killer; she really believed it had been Mr. and Mrs. Dragstedt who had killed their own son. But no evidence supported her theory and their alibies were waterproof. They had the plane tickets to prove it and even surveillance cameras from the place in France where they were staying. Maya still couldn't let the thought go, that they might have somehow tricked the system and fabricated the alibis. Could they have done that?

But what about the others? What about Vincent and Susan? Could they have tried to kill them too? And why would they? They had nothing to do with why they wanted to kill Asgar. Maybe he had told them? No, Asgar never spoke to people like Susan or Vincent. One was known as a crackhead or druggie, whereas the other was just known as a cuckoo. Everyone at the school knew that Vincent wasn't well. He believed in all these conspiracy theories and was one step away from wearing a tinfoil hat.

There was no way a boy like Asgar would speak to those two or tell them secrets about himself that he didn't even tell Maya. It made no sense.

That evening, Maya gained access to Asgar's computer once again. She liked to do it because it made her feel like he was still alive, like he was still a real person and not some corpse in the ground.

The same question kept lingering in her mind and she couldn't escape it. Why would they empty his body of blood? Why would anyone do that? Just for the fun of it?

If it was the same killer, then this person had done it to three people so far. The blood had to have some sort of importance, right?

Maya went through his emails once again, then his Skype, his Twitter, Instagram, and Facebook. She lingered on his pictures, especially the ones of her and him together. He had always placed a little heart underneath them. Maya chuckled when remembering one of them and the day it was taken. It was a warm summer day—well, as warm as they get in Denmark—and he had taken her out on his family's boat. It was a great afternoon where they went swimming in the freezing water. Suddenly, she remembered something else about that day. She remembered sensing that something had changed about him, he was acting strangely. Was he scared back then? Was he already afraid and did he know he was in danger?

When she really thought about it, he had acted a little strange all through the fall. Maybe he knew what was going to happen? Had he gotten himself involved in something that he didn't tell her about? Something bad that ended up getting him killed?

Maya opened his calendar and went through his appointments, when she stumbled upon one that had started at the end of summer and gone on for one Thursday afternoon every month after that. It didn't say what it was, only showed an address on every third Thursday of the month.

Chapter 50

I DROVE Victor to Fishy Pines the next day. I felt awful pulling him away from Skye, who was crying like she thought she would never see him again. I told Victor to explain to her that he was coming back, that he would only be gone for a few hours. I think he managed to get her to calm down. I left her with my parents, and Dr. and Mrs. Williamsen were also there, taking care of Susan, who had improved even more and even opened her eyes for a few seconds this morning, but only for a few seconds. Still, it was major progress and Dr. Williamsen was very positive and enthusiastic. He had to go see other patients as well later today, so he would leave Mrs. Williamsen in charge. I had to admit, I didn't mind having them at the house. They were quite a nice couple and I enjoyed talking to them in the evenings. Morten had been so busy I had hardly seen him since I brought in Susan. They still hadn't found Susan's mother and I knew it was bothering him. My guess was he was out there driving around searching for her, asking every drunk in town where she could be.

"I don't want to go to Fishy Pines," Victor said when we drove off.

"I know," I said. "I know you like to hang out with Skye, but you gotta go to school; otherwise, I am going to get in trouble. If I don't take you there, they'll tell me you have to come live there to make sure you get the right help and education you need."

Victor grumbled under his breath while staring out the window. "I don't like it there."

"I thought you loved it," I asked, baffled. "You told me you liked it the last time you were there. I thought you liked to be with kids that were more like you?"

"They're nothing like me. Skye is like me. Skye is just like me."

I took a turn, then stopped at a red light. "You do realize that she can't stay with us forever, don't you?"

"Why not?"

"Because she has a family somewhere. I need to tell Morten soon and then he will have to find her parents."

"She doesn't have any parents," he said. "She told me."

"Is she an orphan? Well then, she must have foster parents, right?" I asked as the light turned green and I continued through our small town. I waved at Mrs. Petersen, who was shoveling snow in front of her house. She waved back.

"I don't know," he said, as usual only answering the first question. I always forgot to only ask him one at a time.

"What's an orphan?"

"Someone who has no parents," I said.

"Then, yes, she is an orphan."

"Okay. But where does she live? Have you talked about that?"

"She's not from around here."

"Well, I think I got that much," I said with a chuckle,

but Victor didn't say anything. He was zoning out as he usually did when he lost interest in the conversation. It especially happened if I used sarcasm. He didn't understand sarcasm at all.

"So, if she isn't from the island, then where is she from?" I asked. "Has she told you anything? Is she from another country?"

He didn't answer. I stopped the car in the parking lot in front of Fishy Pines. "Victor," I said. "We need to find her family and I am counting on you to help me. What language do you speak when you talk with one another in your minds?"

He shrugged. "We just talk."

"All right," I said and got out of the car.

Victor got out as well. His hair could use a brush and a cut. He didn't want me to touch it and it was rare for me to be able to lure him to the hairdresser since he hated the way they touched him. For a long time, I had just cut it while he was asleep, but the result was terrible. I don't think he cared much, though. Except lately when spending time with Skye, I had noticed he had actually brushed it a few times, and once I even saw that he had combed it back using a little water. Today, it was back to its old self, though. And so was Victor. I had enjoyed the past days when he had been with Skye. He had been so happy and even smiling and sometimes he even looked me in the eyes. But now, he was back to his old self.

HP came out to greet us as we entered the building. "Let's start in my office, shall we?"

Chapter 51

"SO, VICTOR," HP said.

We were in his office, sitting on a set of soft couches. The walls had colorful paintings. There were plants and stress balls on the floor and a soft carpet that toys could get lost in. On the couches were pillows, many pillows you could hug if you got sad, I imagined.

HP was wearing a knitted sweater with a snowman on it, and his beard was long and movements slow as he leaned back on his couch. It was all very relaxed, or at least he wanted it to seem that way. To me, it was everything but.

"Doctor, we…"

"Please, call me HP. I've told you that before, Emma. It's okay. Everyone else calls me that around here," he said with a smile on his pale face. He was very blond, almost an albino, and his skin was pink and seemed irritated. It was scaling in patches on his neck and hands.

"Okay, HP," I said, still not comfortable calling him that. I liked the fact that he was trying hard to not be *doctor-*

like, to make the kids feel like it was a normal school and not a hospital, but still. It was strange somehow.

"Victor didn't feel well for a few days. I'm sorry it came right at the beginning of his time here, but I didn't want him to give it to everyone else here, if you know what I mean."

"Yes, and no, of course not. But I'm just making sure we're on the same page here," he said, leaning forward, rubbing his hands together. Some dry skin fell off and landed in the thick carpet.

HP noticed that I cringed, then chuckled. "I am sorry. It's this cold weather. Makes my eczema flare up."

He walked to the desk, grabbed a bottle of moisturizer from the drawer, and massaged its content into his hands and face, making a squishing sound that made me cringe again.

"So darn hard to keep it moist this time of year, right? I keep using all this moisturizer, but little does it help."

I nodded. I didn't have eczema myself but knew others who did. I knew it could be very annoying and bothersome. I did, however, suffer from dry skin like most people around here.

"It has been unusually cold," I said. "And dry."

"It sure has," he said and sat back down. "All right. So just to be sure, everything is all right, right? We didn't do anything or say anything to make you keep him home?"

"No, nothing like that at all. No. I mean…he has been happy here so far…it's just, well…Victor just needed a break."

HP's eye twitched. "I thought he was sick?"

"He was…just…he needed a break to be sick in. That's all. He's fine now, right buddy?"

Victor didn't say anything. He wasn't interested in talking to HP, so he just didn't. He had no social skills whatsoever. That meant no empathy to make him want to have people like him or make them feel good in his presence. Sometimes, I thought it had to be very liberating to just not care what people thought.

"Great," HP said, smiling. "Here's the deal. We have put together a plan for him based on what little we know. Nothing is set in stone, and it can change with time. In it, we have set some goals that we believe we can reach together. But it requires your full support and help because we can't do it alone. I have it all in this folder, along with the assessment we made on his first days here. Go over them and let me know if you have any concerns. Anything at all. I would love to hear them, all right? And Victor, I can't tell you how happy we are to have you here."

Victor didn't answer, but HP didn't seem to mind. He was probably used to it. I grabbed the folder from his hand and shivered a little when I spotted the scaly skin his hands had left on top of it, then forced a smile.

"I'll go through this and let you know."

"Excellent," HP said.

As we exited the office, Victor's teacher, Victoria Kristensen stood outside, waiting. She smiled.

"I'll walk you to class, Victor."

I walked with them since the entrance was that way anyway, but as we trotted down the hallway, Victor suddenly stopped.

"What's wrong, buddy?" I asked.

He didn't answer. I noticed that his hands were shaking, his fists clenched so hard his knuckles were turning white.

"Oh, my," Mrs. Kristensen said. "Is he having a fit?"

I looked at my son, then bent down in front of him. "I think he's hearing something," I said and looked around me, searching for whatever could have scared him. There was a door next to where he had stopped that said NO ENTRY.

"That door. Where does it lead?"

"It leads to the old part of the building. We don't use it anymore," Mrs. Kristensen said. "There used to be a department for adult patients, but it was closed down many years ago, back in the eighties, as a matter of fact. Now, we only focus on the children. The building is condemned and should be torn down, but I guess they haven't been able to get the funds to do it. You know how it is."

Victor was shaking heavily now. His entire body was trembling, his lips quivering.

"It's okay, Vic," I said. "There's nothing there." I turned to look at Mrs. Kristensen. "Sometimes, he can hear the pipes from the sewer, and hear the noise they make and it scares him. Especially when they freeze."

"Oh, well, we have a lot of that here," she answered. "It's an old building, you know."

"Yes, I know," I said. "It's all over the island. He hears it more often than I do, and for some reason, it scares him."

Mrs. Kristensen smiled and nodded, looking like she genuinely cared.

"Maybe he hears things louder than most of us; it's not uncommon in children with borderline autism. They're more sensitive to sounds. We'll work on his anxieties. It'll get better. HP does wonders with these kids. Just you wait and see."

Chapter 52

I HAD coffee with Sophia and we sat in the kitchen while Mrs. Williamsen took care of Susan in my living room. My parents grabbed a cup with us, while Skye was drawing on a sketchpad I had given her.

"So, what are you going to do about her?" my mother asked, whispering and pointing.

"You don't have to whisper, Mom," I said. "She doesn't understand what we say."

"Right," my mom said, holding her cup between her hands. She had brought her own almond milk to put in it and told me we could just leave it here in my fridge for the next time she came around.

"And to answer your question, I don't know."

"She still hasn't told Morten," Sophia said.

"You what?" my mom said, appalled.

"I HAVEN'T TOLD HIM," I said loudly like she was deaf. I was mocking her, and she knew it. She made a face and shook her head.

"Why haven't you told him?" my dad asked.

"She's afraid he might take her away," Sophia said.

"Hey, I can answer for myself, thank you. But, yes, that is why," I said, slurping my coffee.

"You can't keep her," my mom said. "They'll think you kidnapped her. Oh, the poor parents."

"She doesn't have any parents," I said.

I grabbed a cookie. Having my mom in the house made me anxious. My mom sent me a glance when I took it and I ate it all in one bite just to annoy her. She rolled her eyes at me. It reminded me of Maya when she was younger. I wondered for a second how she was doing in school today.

"How do you know?" my mom asked.

"She told Victor."

"So, she does talk?"

"Nope."

My mom sighed. "Would you stop with all the riddles? How do you know she doesn't have any parents?"

"I told you. She told Victor."

"Are you even listening to this?" she said, addressed to my dad. He gave me a look that told me to be nice.

"How could she tell Victor if she can't speak our language?" he asked.

"They speak. Sort of."

"In their minds," Sophia said, touching her temples with her pointers and making crazy eyes.

"I don't understand anything of what you two are saying," my mom said and threw out her hands.

My dad seemed to get it. He looked at me. "So, you don't think anyone is looking for her?"

I shrugged. "I haven't found anyone. No one in Denmark is looking for a girl of her description, no."

"I still think you should tell Morten," my dad said.

"And risk the girl becoming a number in the system, maybe even a guinea pig?" Sophia asked, horrified.

"Oh," my mom squealed. "I'm gonna be on the news, aren't I? I can see the headlines already. Crazy lady kidnaps child and holds her captive. Her mother finally speaks out."

I pointed at my mother. "Don't you dare speak out to the media."

I felt my phone vibrate in my pocket and took it out. It was Fishy Pines. Heart in my throat, I picked it up. It was Victor's teacher.

"There has been an incident. You should come."

Chapter 53

MRS. KRISTENSEN WAS WAITING for me by the entrance of the school, looking all flustered. Her eyes were avoiding mine, her hands shaking, and she was mumbling under her breath. She was rushing ahead of me down the hallway, her heels clicking on the floors.

"It was one of the other children. He took a book from Victor, pulled it out from between his hands, and then… well, Victor got really angry and…well…I didn't exactly see how it happened because it all went so fast…it was really fast…"

She hurried to the classroom and stopped by the open door.

"What was fast? What happened?" I asked.

"Maybe it's best you see for yourself," she said and led me into the classroom. I walked in, then almost dropped my purse.

"Victor did…that?"

Mrs. Kristensen nodded with a small whimper. "I-It was like an explosion. That's how it felt. Like pressure rushing through the room. It hurt our ears. Next thing, all the windows simply popped. Glass was everywhere, as you can see. It was flying through the air. We were lucky that no one was hit by it. Most of it landed on the outside."

"You're telling me that my son…Victor…got angry and then…exploded all four windows? How?"

She looked at me, terrified. "T-that's what we don't really know."

I stared at the glass on the floor. "But no one was hurt?"

She shook her head. "Luckily, no."

"And where are the children now?"

"We had to move them to another classroom. Victor is with HP. In his office. Waiting for you. I'll take you to see him."

I followed Mrs. Kristensen down the hallway to HP's office. Victor was standing facing the window when I came inside. HP got up from the couch when he saw me.

"He hasn't said a word to me," he said.

"Victor?" I said and walked up to him. I stood behind him, not quite knowing how to approach this situation. I had been through this before. I had received many calls from his old school, but that was usually because Victor had thrown some sort of fit, never because he had destroyed something or even tried to hurt anyone. Victor wasn't violent.

"Victor, buddy? Are you all right?"

He didn't answer. "What happened?" I continued, trying to get his attention. "Why did you get angry?"

"He took my book," Victor said. "I wasn't done with it. You can't just take a book when someone isn't done with it."

I exhaled, trying to not lose my cool. This was tough. "I understand that you got angry," I said. "But how did you break all those windows?"

Victor shook his head. "I don't know."

I nodded, thinking it made sense. Victor had done this without realizing it was going to happen.

"He didn't mean to…" I said, turning to face HP.

HP raised his hand. "I know. We know. It just happened. But you must understand that we can't have him in the same room as other students. At least not for now. It's not safe."

"Of course not, so what do you want us to do?" I asked, worrying that we were back to homeschooling.

"I'll work with him," HP said. "I think Victor and I can get really far if we work together, what do you say, Victor?"

He didn't answer. None of us expected him to. HP put his hand on my shoulder. It was glistening with moisturizer.

"He's a very special boy, Emma. And I have a feeling we haven't seen all of what he is capable of."

"He has been doing things lately that I…I don't know how to describe them."

"Try anyway."

"Like making things float," I said, feeling like I was betraying my son. "I have no idea how to handle it, to be honest."

HP nodded. "He is developing his skills. Probably because he is approaching puberty. We just need to find a way to help him control it. If you'll let me work with him. I find him very interesting. Very, very interesting."

Chapter 54

I TOOK VICTOR HOME. Skye was standing in the hallway when I opened the door, like she knew we were coming. She ran to him and hugged him. Victor hugged her back, much to my surprise, even with a smile.

I missed hugging him and holding him tight like that and I wished he would let me.

The two of them took off into the living room and I walked in after them to see what they were up to, but all I saw were the two of them sitting on their knees on the carpet, staring into each other's eyes. I could tell they were communicating somehow, but they were just sitting there, completely still. It was odd, and I felt left out.

I glanced at Susan who was still out, and Mrs. Williamsen was sitting in a chair next to her, knitting. I smiled and waved at her, then went to the kitchen where Sophia was still sitting, sipping coffee and reading the paper.

"Your parents left about half an hour ago, but I thought I'd stay and keep an eye on that girl for you."

I grabbed the pot and poured myself a cup. "Thank you."

"She didn't do anything weird, just drew a bunch of drawings," Sophia said, her nose in the paper. "How did it go with Victor?"

I sighed. "Not good. Apparently, he shattered four windows."

Sophia looked up from her paper. "You're kidding me? Victor? He would never do something like that. Victor isn't violent. He won't even fight like my boys do. He wouldn't hurt a fly."

"Well, apparently, he did it…he shattered those windows…with his mind somehow."

"What?"

I exhaled deeply and threw out my arms, resigned. "I don't know what is going on, Sophia. Sometimes I think I'm just losing my mind. I think it might have to do with Skye. You know how he has always been strange and could see and hear things I couldn't. Even sometimes warn me about the future?"

"Yes."

"Well, I think his powers are evolving. I think Skye opened a door to him somehow. To what he is capable of. Made him come out of his shell, in a sense."

I looked at the pile of drawings, wondering if there might be anything in them that could help me, anything to tell me where Skye came from or where she belonged.

I grabbed the first one. It was a drawing of a big fat rat. It was very accurate and drawn very detailed, but creepy. I grabbed the next and spotted another rat, just like the first one. The third showed just another rat and so did the fourth and fifth. I threw them all back in the pile with a sigh. This was getting me nowhere.

"I need more coffee," I said and walked to the pot. It

was empty, so I made a fresh one, then grabbed some cookie dough from the fridge and made a batch of cookies on a sheet and put them in the oven.

"I'm making the kids some lunch. You want something to eat?" I asked.

"Herring on rye-bread, please," she said. "If you're having some anyway, that is."

"Of course. I'll go ask the kids what they want to eat," I said.

I stepped into the living room, searching for the kids, when I spotted them over by Susan. Mrs. Williamsen was there too.

"What's going on?" I asked.

"It's a miracle," Mrs. Williamsen said. "She woke up. Come."

I approached the couch. Susan had her eyes open and was smiling. "Oh, my," I said and clasped my mouth.

Mrs. Williamsen brought Susan a glass of water and helped her drink it. "There you go. Small sips."

Victor and Skye laughed and giggled, then rose to their feet, grabbed their jackets, and ran outside to play in the yard. I was about to yell after them that they had to get some lunch first, but I never got to it since I was so over-whelmed. Not only had Susan woken up, but I had just heard my son giggle and laugh for the first time in as long as I could remember.

"It was truly strange," Mrs. Williamsen said. "I was sitting and knitting when the girl walked to Susan and put her hand on her forehead. I didn't notice at first, but as soon as I did, I tried to stop her, and that was when I suddenly realized that Susan had opened her eyes. The kids were so excited. They're so sweet, the two of them. They have a truly special friendship."

I sighed and walked to the window. I spotted the two of

them engaged in some game out by the tall trees. Victor was making a snowball and throwing it at her, making it float in front of her first, then as she turned around, he made it smash into her face. Skye, in return, jumped up high, higher than what seemed humanly possible, grabbed one of the tall branches and rustled it till it dropped a bunch of snow on top of Victor. Then they both laughed, Skye still floating in the air above him.

"They sure do," I mumbled under my breath, worrying about the day she wouldn't be here anymore. It was going to kill Victor.

Chapter 55

MAYA WAS FREEZING and blowing on her hands to keep them warm. She and Samuel had been waiting outside the house for an hour now. They didn't know what exactly they were waiting for, but something.

"Are you sure it's here?" Samuel asked.

"This is the address from Asgar's calendar," she said, her lips quivering, her breath crystallizing in front of her. It was dark out and the house looked warm and cozy with all the lights on inside.

"And you're sure it was today and at this time?"

"It was on the calendar from six to seven, so I don't know if it was six or seven o'clock," she said.

Samuel nodded and jumped up and down a few times to get warmer. Maya did the same.

"If nothing happens at seven o'clock, then we leave," he said.

"Yes. It's probably just a wild shot, but I felt like we had to at least check it out," she said.

"Wait…something is happening," he said.

Someone on a bike rode up in front of the house, then parked it outside and went in.

"Maybe he lives there," Maya said.

"Yeah, probably," Samuel said, blowing on his hands. Even though they were wearing mittens, it was still too cold.

"You think that guy lives there too?" Maya asked as someone else walked up the driveway and entered the house through the front door.

Samuel shrugged. "Maybe."

"And that woman?" Maya pointed at a woman who parked her car in the driveway and rushed into the house. None of them even knocked. They all acted like they were very familiar with the house.

"Maybe it's like a meeting or something?" Maya asked.

"What? Like AA?"

"Yes."

"I hardly think Asgar was a drunk," Samuel said.

"Maybe it's for something else. Like a support group."

Samuel nodded. "You wanna go and see?"

Maya smiled. "Sure."

They walked across the street and up to the house, then paused by the front door just as some other guy showed up behind them and walked right in. They followed him, staying close behind him.

Inside were about twenty people gathered in the living room. They were drinking coffee and tea and talking to each other. In the middle of the living room, there was a circle of chairs. On the wall behind a big muscular guy was a poster with a big light blob in a dark sky. On it was written FANOE ISLAND UFO RESEARCH and EXPERIENCERS GROUP.

Maya looked at Samuel, then back at the group, who had now seen them and stopped their chatting.

"Ah, newcomers," someone said.

Maya turned around and looked into the face of a very pale man with ruby red lips. He reached out his hand toward hers and she took it, even though the skin on it was flaky and peeling off in patches. It was also peeling on his face and throat, even though he tried to cover it up by wearing a turtleneck.

"Welcome to our club. My name is Thomas. We'll share our experiences in just a few minutes, as soon as everyone is here. We're so excited to have you here."

Chapter 56

"WE ARE ACTUALLY HERE to talk about our friend, Asgar Dragstedt."

Maya looked around at the many faces staring at her. The meeting had been going on for about half an hour and she had been listening to one story after another about alien abductions and UFO sightings, and now it was her turn to share her extraterrestrial story, as Thomas had put it.

The room went silent. A few looks were exchanged, but no one said anything. "He was found in the dunes recently," Maya continued. "Dead."

Thomas looked at her, then sighed. "Yes, well. We all heard about that. And we all fear ending up like him. He's the fourth of our members to disappear over the past few months."

Maya's eyes grew wide. "Four? Four of your members have disappeared?"

Thomas nodded. "Yes."

"People usually only disappear for a few hours at a

time," a woman sitting next to him said. "You know, when they're…taken. But lately, they haven't been coming back."

"We fear we might be next," a man sitting across from her said.

"Who else are you missing?" Samuel asked.

"Is Susan Ludvigsen one of them?" Maya asked.

They looked at one another. Thomas then nodded. "Yes, she used to come here too."

"But she is a hothead," Samuel said. "She does mushrooms and smokes a lot of pot; how can you believe anything she says?"

"Because she shared a story with so many others," Thomas said. "Susan's story was the same as Asgar's."

"What?" Maya said. "What story?"

"Susan, Asgar, Tim, and Vincent all came here in July with the same story. They had been at a party at the end of the school year in June and had a bonfire down on the beach. They had been drinking and partying along with a bunch of other kids from their school when suddenly, a bright light had enveloped them. The four of them had all been taken away and had experiments performed on them. The rest of the partygoers didn't experience anything. Or they didn't see what happened. They don't know. The next thing they remember is waking up on the north end of the island, in the forest between tall trees, naked. They all had the same two red injection marks on their arms. They all felt strange afterward. It was Asgar who came first after he had accidentally hurt himself horseback riding. It was just a scratch, but that was when he saw it and that was what brought him here. Soon after, the others came as well. They believed they had been abducted that night and experimented on. They are not the only ones. All of us here share the same story. People from all over the island come here, especially young teens. Even all the way from Sonderho."

"Saw what?" Maya asked. "I don't understand. What did he see?"

They exchanged glances once again, then Thomas spoke. "His blood. It had changed."

Maya looked at Samuel. This was going too far, she thought to herself. These guys were nothing but lunatics.

Thomas rolled his sleeve up and walked to the kitchen, grabbed a knife, and brought it back. He cut himself on the arm with it and Maya winced.

"Don't do that," she said.

"No," he said. "I want you to see this. Look."

Maya stared at the wound where blood was now oozing out. Only it wasn't blood the way she knew blood. This wasn't crimson red. This was more like a dark yellow.

"Asgar had the same blood," Thomas said. "That's what they have done to us. They injected their blood into us. We think it might be because they're creating a mixture of our blood and theirs, you know, because otherwise, they can't survive here on our earth once they come down here. This way, they mix our blood with theirs, then drain it from us again and inject it into their soldiers. They're preparing to take over and when they do, we'll be nothing but a blood bank for their survival. Asgar was the first. Vincent is still in the hospital because they almost drained him too. They're coming for us. It won't be long now. The question is, are YOU ready for contact?"

Part V

TWO DAYS LATER

Chapter 57

SUSAN BLINKED HER EYES. She didn't quite know where she was or even who she was. She had been in this strange place for a few days since she woke up and, even though they tried and tried to get her to remember, she simply couldn't.

She had learned that her name was Susan and that the house she was in belonged to this woman named Emma. She didn't know where she knew her from, but she did remember her face, sort of. At least she believed she did. There was something familiar about it.

There was a man who came to her every day. His name was Morten Bredballe, he told her. He was asking her a lot of questions, but she couldn't answer most of them. At least not in a way he wanted her to. It was obvious that he felt disappointed every time and she didn't like that. Susan didn't like to disappoint anyone.

Now, he was here again, sitting next to her on the couch, looking confused, rubbing his hair.

"Let's try again, Susan," he said.

Susan. She tasted the word. It had such a strange ring to it.

"Do you remember anything about where you were while you were gone? Were you in a house?"

Susan sighed and tried to remember, but she was completely blank. She shook her head.

"No, you weren't in a house or no you don't remember?" he asked.

She shrugged. "I don't know."

"Okay. Okay. Do you remember any faces, anyone who was with you?" he asked.

He had asked her that one before, but apparently not been very satisfied with the answer.

"I don't know," she said.

"Someone took your blood," he said. "While you were gone. You came back here almost drained. Do you remember who did that to you?"

Susan looked at him. She tried to look like she was thinking about it, but really, she wasn't because there was nothing there. Absolutely nothing. It was all just darkness.

Officer Morten Bredballe sighed. "I'm guessing you still don't know."

"I'm sorry," she said.

The woman, Emma, stepped forward. "Don't be, sweetie. It's not your fault. You're doing the best you can. You were out for quite some time."

"How about the cabin we found you in? The guy who owns it says he went back to his house north of Copenhagen and his surveillance cameras show you walking in the front door two days before Emma found you. He told us he has been having problems with the lock, so that was why you found it open. Do you remember anything before getting to that cabin? How far did you run?"

She stared at him, not knowing what to say.

"This is hopeless," he said. "Can't you at least remember something? A face, a name, something?"

Emma gave Morten a look. "It's not her fault she can't remember. You can't force it out of her," she said.

He got up. "Maybe she was just doing drugs. And maybe the Dragstedts did kill their son."

"How do you suffer blood loss by doing drugs? Huh? And how do you explain Vincent?" Emma asked.

Morten exhaled and ran a hand through his hair again. "Yeah, you're right. It's just…so frustrating. I can't get anything out of any of them. Vincent is still out and this one…this one can't…remember a darn thing. How am I supposed to get anywhere with this case?"

Emma smiled and put her arm around his shoulder.

"With lots of coffee," she said and took him into the kitchen.

Susan sat for a little while staring at the living room in front of her. She liked it here. She didn't know anything else so far, but she knew she liked it. She didn't even remember her own home or her mother, whom they kept talking about. Apparently, she had been found in some alley. An overdose they called it, not that Susan knew what that was, but she wasn't here anymore they said. Susan knew she was supposed to feel sad about that, but since she couldn't remember her, she found it hard to cry over her. They had to figure out what to do with her. She needed a guardian, they said.

Susan sighed and looked around when suddenly she heard a sound, a whistling that was familiar to her. She almost gasped in excitement and turned towards it. She knew that whistling from somewhere. And that song. She knew it.

Waltzing Matilda, was it…right? It was the first thing she knew for certain that she remembered since she woke up. It was coming from the window behind her. Outside was someone, a man. He was whistling and waving at her.

Susan waved back.

Chapter 58

I POURED MORTEN SOME COFFEE. He sighed and rubbed his stubble. "I don't know what to do here, Emma. I'm beginning to think I'm going crazy. This story makes no sense whatsoever."

I nodded and poured myself some coffee, then sat down. "Honey, you have hardly slept since we found Asgar's body. Don't you think it would be good for you to get some sleep? It might help you think more clearly."

He nodded. "I know. I just keep thinking about these kids, you know? I want to find whoever did this to them. I keep thinking about Jytte and Maya and all the other kids and who might be next. You should see that Vincent kid; he's like a withered flower. I can't risk any more of them ending up like him. I simply can't."

I sipped my coffee and thought about Maya. I was happy she was hanging out with Samuel a lot, at least she had someone to protect her in case this creep showed up and picked her next.

"At least Susan is safe and doing a lot better," I said, grabbing his hand in mine.

"True. But now there's the issue of her mother and finding a place for Susan to live."

"She can stay here as long as she likes."

"You sure?"

"Absolutely. I have plenty of room. I've given her one of the rooms upstairs, but she feels more comfortable on the couch, she says. Once she gets tired of Victor and Skye, she has a room waiting for her."

"What's up with that girl anyway?" Morten suddenly asked.

My heart pounded. I looked away. "I…what do you mean?"

"She's been here for weeks now. Where are her parents?"

"They're having trouble," I said. "Why? Have you heard anything? Is anyone searching for her maybe?" I asked, laughing awkwardly.

He shook his head. "No, of course not. But if they keep having problems, we might want to involve social services. She might need a foster home if they can't provide a home for her."

"Of course," I said. "Or she could just stay here."

Morten exhaled. "Emma?"

"Yes?"

"You do know the parents, right?"

"Well…how do you define knowing them?"

"As in you have met them?"

"Well…not actually…met them…"

"Emma!"

"What?"

Morten looked at me angrily. "Are you telling me you're keeping a girl here and you don't know where she belongs?"

I bit my lip. "Maybe a little bit."

"Emma!"

"What? No one is looking for her. She says she doesn't have any parents." He gave me a very stern look.

"I'm sorry," I said. "But you've seen the two of them together. They've bonded. Actually bonded. Victor has never bonded with anyone his own age before. He's never been this happy, nor has he ever been this well. Please, don't take her away from us. Please, don't call social services. I'll adopt her if possible. "

He sighed. "I am sorry, Emma. I know you mean well. But she needs to go back where she came from. I'll let you keep her until I find another solution, but then she's out of here. You hear me? You can't just keep some random girl in your house, Emma. Where is your head at?"

Morten rose to his feet and looked at his watch. "I gotta go. I have a meeting with the colleagues from Copenhagen at the station in a few minutes. I have to be there to make sure they don't totally mess this entire case up." He leaned over and kissed me on the lips. "Be good, Emma. Don't get yourself into more trouble, will you promise me that? Please?"

I made a grimace. "I am not sure I can."

"Emma."

"All right. All right. Geez. I will. I will stay out of trouble."

Chapter 59

MAYA STARED at the computer screen. She had been going through article after article on obscure web pages about UFO sightings and reading through testimony after testimony in online support groups. Still, it made no sense to her. She was on the phone with Samuel, while reading some of it out loud for him.

"Take this one, for example. She believes she was taken into a spacecraft where she helped create some sort of alien hybrids with some of her eggs. 'They chose me,' she writes. She also goes on to say that she doesn't very often share her story because most people aren't ready for that information yet. She doesn't want to freak people out."

Samuel chuckled on the other end. Maya felt so confused.

"Why do you think Asgar went to these meetings?" she asked.

"Maybe he really did experience something," Samuel answered.

"So, you actually think he was sucked into a spaceship and that they performed some sort of experiment on him, doing what? Changing out his blood like that guy claimed?"

"I know it sounds absurd, but knowing Asgar, he must have experienced something that night. He would never make something like that up. It's very unlike him. Asgar was a smart kid."

Maya sighed. She knew Samuel was right. Susan, she could understand. Susan could have experienced all sorts of things in that drugged out mind of hers. But Asgar? Asgar was a good kid from a nice family. He might have a drink every now and then when they partied, but he was never drunk out of his mind like most teenagers around there. He preferred to stay clear in his mind and he didn't like to lose control, he once told her. That was part of why Maya enjoyed his company so much. He wasn't like the others. She could hang with him and not be bored at a party while the rest of them got drunk and unpleasant. They could be together and laugh at the rest of them acting crazy.

"Could he have been drunk?" Maya still asked. "When he believed he experienced those things?"

"I don't know. Asgar didn't drink, usually."

"But maybe he did that time," Maya said.

"You're thinking that maybe it was around the same time he found out about his real mother? That maybe he needed to drink to forget? I don't know. I guess it is possible."

"And what about that blood thing? Do you buy into that?" Maya asked. "It seemed pretty far out to me."

"Yeah. Me too. But still. We saw it with our own eyes. Whatever came out of that guy wasn't normal blood if you ask me."

"He could have a disease or something," Maya said, scrolling through a new article. "Maybe it was a trick."

Samuel went quiet for a few seconds, and Maya read another article. "Do you believe in UFOs?" she finally asked.

Sam was still quiet. "I don't think we're alone in the universe. I do believe some people have experienced things, odd things from other planets or other universes parallel to ours. So, yes, technically you could say I believe in it. I mean, how would you explain so many similar stories coming from all over the world?"

Maya sighed and leaned back in her chair. It protested by squeaking. "I guess I believe a little too," she said. "Maybe. I mean…I believe there is more to the world than what we can see. Lately, things have been kind of odd around here, with my brother's weird friend and all. I guess I've realized there is more between heaven and earth."

"I'm sure there's a lot we just don't know or understand."

Maya looked out the window. She had slept in today since it was Saturday, but that meant it was already the afternoon. At this time of year, it got dark at four o'clock and the light was already dimming. She wondered if the sun had even been out at all today, if it had been able to break through the heavy, thick, dark clouds.

"I can't wait to see you. When will you be here?"

"Oh, I already am. I'm right outside your house."

Chapter 60

I HAD BEEN WRITING QUITE a lot lately and now, when Morten left, I turned to my laptop to do some research. The story was beginning to unfold about the wealthy family and their secrets, but I still didn't believe they had killed Asgar. Therefore, I got stuck with finding out the rest of the story. I wanted to know more about the family and especially the golf course back when it first opened, so I turned to the local library and their online archives. I found some old articles from 1901 about the grand opening of the first golf course in Denmark. Even the royal family and King Christian the 9th were present. It was quite an event for the small island.

I read through the old article about the new pride of the town and how the Dragstedts believed it would attract tourists to the island. Most islanders had their concerns about the tourists because, what it would do to the island's beautiful nature, especially the Wadden Sea with its shallow body of water, tidal flats, and wetlands? Plus, the infrastructure on the island was barely able to cope with as many people as were there. This was a place for fishermen.

"Why would tourists want to come to this desolate and windy place?" one of the locals was quoted saying. "We have nothing but smelly fish and empty beaches here."

"That golf course will be closed within the year," someone else was quoted saying.

I chuckled, thinking, if only they had known. Not only was the golf course still running, it was a very profitable business. And now, years later, tourism was actually Fanoe Island's main industry. Every year, we received more than thirty-thousand visitors, and they especially came because of the wide beaches, where they could do all kinds of water sports like kite flying, surfing, and driving those annoying beach buggies in the sand. It was fun to think about how the Dragstedt family had actually been the first to see this potential, even though, back then, they believed it was the idea of a madman.

But as I was busy indulging in the history of our small island, I came across a picture in one of the articles that immediately made me stop and stare, almost dropping my coffee cup. I zoomed into it, to better see because I simply couldn't believe it. It was pixelated; still, I had no problem seeing what—or who—it was.

"How on earth is that possible?" I asked, staring at the man. "This picture is more than a hundred years old."

I scrolled down the article and found another picture from that same day and there he was again. Dressed as a nobleman.

Maybe it's a relative?

I heard Maya on the stairs, then the front door open, and guessed Samuel had to be here. I had told her to stop having him climb up the ladder when we all knew he was there anyway. She opened the front door and I heard voices speaking in the hallway.

I looked at the screen and the picture, then back at the door to the kitchen, listening to the voices behind it. I heard them walk into the living room and that was when it hit me.

I grabbed the computer, got up, and ran out.

Chapter 61

I FOUND ALL of them in the living room. Victor and Skye were sitting by the window, a ball floating between them, probably engaged in some odd conversation I would never be a part of.

Maya and Samuel were standing by Susan, who was sitting on the couch, looking at Samuel, her eyes glistening with excitement.

They turned around when I walked in.

"What's going on?" I asked, approaching them cautiously.

"Nothing, Mom," Maya said. "Samuel is just saying hi to Susan."

"I remember him," Susan said, smiling blissfully while looking up at Samuel. "I actually remember him. I can't remember where from, but I know that I remember him."

"Well, that's great," I said as I looked at the screen in my hand, then back up at Samuel.

"It was the song," Susan said. "The song he was whistling. I recognized it and that's how I realized that I knew him from somewhere."

I sighed. "That's awesome, Susan. I'm glad you're beginning to remember things."

"That's a good sign, right?" she asked.

I nodded. "It sure is. Say, Samuel, I thought you said you and your family came to the island just a few years ago?"

He nodded. "Yes. We came from Copenhagen. I was born there and most of my family still lives there."

"Really?" I asked. "And you don't have any ancestors that used to live here on the island?"

He shook his head, looking a little confused. His eyes settled on Victor and Skye, who didn't seem interested in what was going on around them. Samuel's hands were clenched into fists. He was shivering slightly as he watched them, even though he was still speaking to me.

"No. I don't think any of us ever came out here, why?"

"It's just…well, I came across this picture here." I turned the laptop around and showed it to Maya and Samuel.

"Wow, that looks just like you, Sam," Maya said.

Samuel stared at the old photo, then up at me, his eye twitching. "Must be a coincidence."

"Really? Is it also a coincidence that this guy has the exact same scar on his cheek as you have? Because, as far as I know, that's not something you inherit from your ancestors. This is you, Samuel. How do you explain that?"

Samuel rubbed his temples while making an aggravated sound. Maya stared at him, startled. She pulled away.

"Samuel? Is my mom right? And what's going on with your hands? And your face? What's happening? Is your eczema acting up again?"

Samuel moved his hands and a big patch of his skin peeled off and fell to the carpet below. Older and more wrinkled skin appeared beneath it, some of it was almost grey and lifeless. Maya screamed.

"Samuel, what's going on here?" she asked, her voice breaking. "What's happening to your skin?"

Susan stood up, then sang. Her voice was eerily shrill, cutting through the tension in the room, "...*And you'll come a-waltzing, Mati-i-i-lda, with me.*"

Her facial expression changed as she sang. From confusion to one of utter terror.

"Now, I remember," she said, gasping to breathe. "You...that song, you whistled it...wearing a mask and..."

"A mask? What is she talking about, Samuel?" Maya shrieked.

I grabbed my daughter and pulled her away from him, while Susan stood frozen and looked like all her memories were coming back at once.

"Samuel is the one who killed Asgar," I said. "He also kept Susan captive and emptied her and Vincent of their blood. You've been around for a very long time, haven't you?"

Samuel smiled, his face cracking as his lips moved. "Yes. I came here centuries ago."

"W-where are you from?" Maya asked.

"Somewhere else," he said. "Somewhere different. A place where there are many like those two." He pointed at Victor and Skye. "A place where their blood can keep me alive. Here, it's different. I came here by accident. I don't know how it happened. All I know is, I was having a blast with my friends, partying, and I woke up in your sewers back when they were newly built. Don't know how I got there and, all this time, I've been looking for a way back. That's why I collect clocks. I am fascinated by time. It passes by outside my house, yet I don't grow older. Meanwhile, I have been living off your filthy blood, while looking for the real deal." He pointed at Skye. "Like hers. If I get some of hers, I'll sleep for decades and wake up younger than I was when I went to sleep. It's very much like winding up a clock. It just keeps ticking, tick-tock, but nothing really changes. They too can stay the same for centuries."

"And every now and then," I said, "you find children like them, like Skye, who come from the same place you do, who accidentally end up here in our world, and you drink their blood and sleep. And then, when you wake up, you start looking for them again."

"Your thin blood only keeps me alive for a few hours, whereas theirs…theirs, boy, it is go-o-o-od."

"Is that why you took Asgar?" Maya asked. "Because his blood had changed?"

Samuel nodded. "Yesss, my dear. I don't know how it happened to him, but I had been awake for two years, and I was craving the good blood, while living off scraps, drinking blood from a few teenagers that no one would miss. I had grabbed them in Sonderho and kept them in my house, but their blood was barely keeping me going. Suddenly, I smelled the good blood on Asgar one day when he cut himself. We were at his house making sandwiches and he cut himself with the knife. The smell wasn't strong, but I immediately knew he had some of our blood mixed in him."

"How?" I asked, baffled. "How did he get different blood?"

"We don't know," Maya said. "He believed he had been taken by a spacecraft and experimented on. That aliens had changed his blood by injecting some of theirs. "

"But, instead, it was blood injected from someone coming from the same place as Samuel came from," I said, not quite sure I believed any of this. But, in a strange way, it made sense.

Maya looked pensive. "So, that was why you took them? Asgar, Susan, and Vincent. They all shared the same story; they all had their blood changed."

"But it wasn't enough," Samuel said. "The concentration was too weak. It helped me for a little while, but it isn't enough." Samuel's skin was sizzling like it was burning, and he grabbed his face in pain.

"I need my mask," he said, "It keeps my face cool and I need…I need blood…" he stared at Skye, his hands shaking. Before I could react, Samuel rushed to Skye, pulled a pocket knife out, and placed it on her throat.

"Hey!" I yelled. "Leave her alone!"

I stepped toward her, but he pressed the knife closer to her skin. "Come any closer and I'll slit her throat," he hissed. "Believe me, I'd love to do just that."

Samuel placed the knife on her arm and cut the skin. Skye cried as blood gushed out. Green, thick blood. Samuel smiled when he saw it, his eyes narrowing, skin peeling off.

"Ah, now that's the right stuff. Not all yellow and mixed like the others were. This is just right. This will keep me alive for decades." He placed his tongue on her skin and licked the green blood. Immediately, his face grew younger and his skin became soft and smooth. He licked his lips with pleasure.

"Let her go," I said.

Samuel hissed at me again, sounding like an angry cat. He grabbed Skye by the throat and lifted her up.

"She's coming with me," he said as he blasted through the French doors faster than I had ever seen anyone run, Skye on his shoulder.

Chapter 62

"WHERE DID HE GO?"

I was immediately after him and out in the yard, but there was no sign of Samuel. I looked at Maya, who had followed me outside.

"How can anyone move that fast?"

"How can anyone do any of the things he just said?" Maya asked.

I looked into her eyes. They were expressing utter terror and devastation.

"I loved him, Mom," she said. "I fell for him. I can't believe the lies he has told me."

I looked around me. It was getting darker. We had to move fast before Samuel started to drink Skye's blood and eventually drained her like he had the others, then went into hibernation.

"Where does he live?" I asked.

Maya stared at me. "Somewhere on the north side of town. I've never been there. No wonder he never wanted me to come to his place or even meet his family. We were always here at our house. I thought he was just being shy."

"Do you know the address?" I asked as we rushed back inside.

Maya shook her head.

"You mean to tell me you've been seeing this guy even though you don't know his address or his parents? Oh, boy, the two of us need to have a talk once this is over. Now, how do we find this place?"

"I might be able to help," Susan said, getting to her feet.

"Susan. Yes, of course," I said. "You've been there. Did he keep you at his house?"

"I think so. It was a very big place. I think I might be able to find it. I remember running through the plantation. He must be on the other side of that."

"Let's go then," I said and shooed the both of them toward the door. "You too, Vic," I said, addressed to the boy who was still sitting by the windowsill staring out the window like he expected Skye to come back any second. I wondered if he even understood what had been going on, what had happened to her.

In the car, I grabbed my phone and called Morten, but he didn't pick up. I left a message while getting the car onto the road.

"We're on our way to the killer's house. Yes, you heard me right. I didn't stay out of trouble, trouble came to me, literally. I know who killed Asgar and took Susan and Vincent, and his name is Samuel," I stopped, realizing I didn't even know the boy's last name. Wow, were we going to do background checks on Maya's boyfriends from now on before letting them come anywhere close to her.

"Anyway, we're on our way there. It's on the north side of the island, behind the plantation. We don't know the exact address yet, but I'll text it or call you again. Did I say it's important that we move fast? He has Skye and wants to…well, take her blood. Call me."

I hung up, pressed the gas pedal down, and rushed through town, secretly hoping a police car would see us and follow. But since the island only had one, it was kind of rare to actually come across it.

Chapter 63

"IT'S OVER THERE, the big one."

Susan pointed out the window. She shivered as she spoke, and I wondered if more memories were coming back to her as she saw the big mansion once again. It was located in one of the most remote areas of the island, and I remember hearing kids tell stories about this estate and how it was haunted by an old vampire. Guess they didn't know how right they were when they came up with that one.

I drove up in front of it and got out.

"You stay here," I told all three of them, especially Victor. He didn't look much like he would go anywhere anyway, so I left them and rushed up to the front door. I grabbed the handle but, of course, it was locked. I called Morten again and left him the address, then called the police station, but the answering machine sent me to Morten's cellphone in case of an emergency. It was late and there was usually just one man on duty at nighttime, so there was no one to answer the phone. If Morten was out on another job or just on patrol, he wouldn't be able to answer.

I grunted angrily, then looked at the door in front of me. How was I supposed to get in? This place was like a fortress, with bars on the windows and everything.

That was when I heard the car door open and shut. I turned and spotted my son walking up the stairs, his raging eyes fixated on the big wooden door.

"Victor? Didn't I ask you to stay in the…?"

He walked past me and up to the door, then threw out his hands and the double doors slammed open with a loud bang.

"I completely forgot he could do that," I said, looking back at Maya, who stared, baffled, from inside the car. "Remind me to tell your sister more about it later," I said to Victor, then walked past the shattered doors.

I followed Victor through the hallway until he stopped in front of a closed door. Again, he lifted his hands and blasted them open. Behind them, we spotted Skye. She was lying in a hospital bed, strapped down and gagged. A tube was already inserted into her vein and the green blood was flowing into a bag.

"Oh, dear God," I said and approached her.

She was making noises behind the gag. I removed it, but whatever came out of her wasn't understandable. I started to unstrap the leather bands, when Victor suddenly said, "Rats."

"What?"

"Rats," he said. "She's showing me pictures of rats. Rats, rats, rats, rats, RATS!"

"What do you mean r…ATS!!"

I turned around just in time to see the wave of rats coming toward us. No, it wasn't a wave, it was a freakin tsunami. Thousands and thousands of rats rushed toward us and, seconds later, knocked us to the floor. They were everywhere. In my clothes, in my hair, and on my back as I tried to get up on my feet. And then I felt the pain as their little teeth pierced my skin and they bit me. As they attacked us, I spotted Samuel standing on the stairs behind them. He had a flute to his lips and was playing *Waltzing Matilda*.

Chapter 64

"HE'S CONTROLLING THEM," I yelled. "Somehow, he is making them do this."

I reached out my hand while lying on the floor, fighting off the rats, trying to grab Victor's hand in mine. He was screaming, fighting a rat biting his earlobe. I used my foot to kick one off my leg, then reached over and slammed the one on Victor's ear, hard, till it flew off and landed up on the wall before it slid down to the floor.

But as soon as it was gone, two more came and bit down on him. He covered his face with his hands and they bit onto his fingers. Victor was screaming loudly. The rats kept coming at us, no matter how much we managed to fight them off. Victor was now completely covered in the furry gray monsters, biting down on him.

"Victor," I yelled, "Victor!"

In the chaos, I managed to look up and notice that Skye had now filled an entire bag with green blood. Samuel approached her, then changed the bag and continued the draining. He put the filled bag on top of another, and I realized he had already taken a lot. Too much for such a young girl. She was lying on the bed, all pale and barely able to keep her eyes open.

"Victor," I yelled through the swarm of rats. "Skye needs help! She needs you! Help her!"

Victor didn't move. He was lying completely still on the floor now, the rats almost covering him from head to toe. My heart sank. Why was he so eerily still? Why had he stopped screaming?

"VICTOR!" I screamed, then reached over with my leg and kicked a few of the rats away from him, but more took their place. It was useless. I could fight them all I wanted to, but there were too many.

One bit down on my lip and I screamed again. I fought it off, frantically hitting it repeatedly until it finally let go of my lip, then I looked over at Victor once again and suddenly saw his back move, raise up, as his body raised to his feet, rats clinging onto him, biting him till blood gushed down his face. Victor didn't even bother to brush them off, he simply bent his head down, then closed his eyes and, seconds later, the first rat popped off his face. Soon, they were flying off one after another, shooting through the room, hitting the walls and floors. As soon as he was clear of them, he lifted all the ones on top of me, pulled them off forcefully using the power of his mind, then had them blast out through the door, shooting like a machine gun.

I looked at my hands, they were bleeding from the many wounds, but the rats were gone. Victor was bleeding too, and that was when I noticed it, noticed what I had never seen before because Victor never got hurt, not even as a young child.

Victor's blood was dark green.

Everything stopped inside of me. I forgot everything about Skye and even Samuel. All I could see was the blood dripping from my son onto the floor. The dark green mass.

"Victor?"

But the boy didn't hear me, nor did he look at me. He only had one thing in mind. And that was saving his best friend.

He bent his head forward, his eyes fixated on Skye and especially Samuel standing next to her. Samuel was staring at him, and especially at the blood on his face. Samuel seemed to be almost in a trance. He walked closer to Victor, reached down with his finger and touched it. Samuel tasted the blood, licking it off his fingertips. Then, he closed his eyes. The skin around them smoothed out, making him look even younger.

"Oh, dear Lord. I mean, I've heard about the dark green blood, but never actually tasted it. I thought it was nothing but an old tale. A myth. But it really exists, doesn't it?"

He caressed Victor's cheek. "You really exist. Just one bag of this blood could keep me alive for a century. It's that powerful."

Samuel grinned, then grabbed Victor by the neck and pressed down, hard. I screamed, so did Victor, but soon the boy fell to his knees, lifeless.

"VICTOR!"

I rushed toward him, but Samuel lifted his hand and, with the force of his hands, threw me back against the wall. It knocked out all the air from my lungs and I slid, paralyzed, to the floor. I could only watch as Samuel grabbed my lifeless boy onto his shoulders and, grinning, ran out of the room.

Chapter 65

WHEN I finally managed to get back on my feet and actually stand up, Victor and Samuel were long gone. I called Victor's name and ran around the house. I ran into each and every room and called for him, but there was no sign of him anywhere. I even ran outside to the car, but Maya and Susan hadn't seen them, they said. I told them to stay in the car since we didn't know if he would come back and it would be very dangerous for them in there if he did, and to keep calling Morten.

I rushed back inside to Skye and took off her straps, then held her in my arms. She already seemed so weak. I looked at her pretty face and moved the hair that had fallen onto it.

"If you in any way can help me, Skye," I said, "then, please, help me find Victor."

Skye looked into my eyes. I could tell she understood what I was saying, but as she opened her mouth to speak, nothing left her lips. I wondered for a second if she was simply not capable of speaking. But then I saw something else that made me completely forget all that. Something quite exceptional.

Inside her very green eyes, I spotted images. It was like a little movie running on repeat. It was showing the same images over and over again. It showed Victor. Victor and Samuel. They were in a dark place, a tunnel of some sort, where there was no light, and Samuel lit their way with his glowing eyes. There was water on the floor. Lots of water.

"The sewer," I said. "He took him into the sewers."

Skye blinked her eyes. A set of stairs was revealed inside her green irises. I had seen those stairs when searching for Victor. I remembered them. They were by the huge kitchen.

"I know where they are," I said, and Skye nodded, then her eyes rolled back in her head and she fell backward onto the bed. She seemed to be sleeping, so I left her there to go and get my son.

I rushed through the kitchen and found the door leading to the stairwell. I had been down there when looking for Victor, but it was so dark down there, I had to give up. Now, I grabbed a flashlight from the kitchen and a knife, then ran down the stony stairway. I ended up in a large room with nothing but an old wooden coffin in the middle of it.

"So, this is where you sleep, huh?" I asked, my voice bouncing off the stone walls. "Kind of cliché, don't ya' think?"

I found another stairwell leading down. I took it and ended up in a room that had a dirt floor. Someone had dug a hole in the middle. I approached the hole through the wet dirt and shone my flashlight into it. I saw water and I saw rats in there. But I also heard something, the sound of something bigger moving down there, feet splashing in the water. And then there was the whistling.

Even though I was still bleeding from my last encounter with the rats, I lowered myself into it, flashlight and knife in my hand, and as my feet landed in the murky water, I set off into the tunnel, following the sound of *Waltzing Matilda.*

Chapter 66

I WAS WALKING in knee-high water and it smelled terrifying. Rats were running above my head on the sides of the walls and I shivered when thinking of their attack earlier. How on earth Samuel managed to make them do what they did was beyond me, but then again, there was a lot lately that was beyond my comprehension.

I didn't have time to focus on that now. All I had on my mind was Victor and getting him back alive, with all his precious blood still inside of him.

I could hear them not too far in front of me and hurried to try and catch up to them, my hand holding the knife in front of me, trembling.

I walked further, then reached a crossroad. I listened to Samuel's whistling, and decided it was coming from the road to the right and followed it, but soon I started to doubt my decision since it sounded like the whistling was getting further and further away. I turned around to walk back when suddenly the whistling stopped. I gasped and stood still for a few seconds, then decided to go back to where I had last heard it. As I turned around, Samuel was right in front of me, his glowing eyes lighting up the darkness.

"Well, hello there."

I screamed. The sound bounced off the walls in the tunnel.

"Where is my son?" I asked, holding out the knife in front of me, trying to seem threatening.

"I don't think he even is your son," Samuel said.

He had some of the dark green blood still on his lips and it angered me so much to think about him drinking my son's blood.

"Of course, he is my son. I gave birth to him, now where is he, you freak of nature? If you hurt him, I will kill you."

I heard a sound that made me turn around. "Is there anyone else down here?" I said.

Samuel laughed. "You still don't understand anything, do you? You silly people."

I turned back and looked at him, pointing the knife at his face, letting it get really close.

"Give. Me. My. Son."

Samuel looked at the knife, then back at me. I pressed it against his throat. "Ha."

He laughed again.

"What's so funny?"

"I don't have time for this," he said, then he blew on me and I flew backward, landing in the water. "You are no match for me."

Samuel walked closer to me, grabbed me by the hair, and lifted me up like I was some doll. He looked down at me, then flipped me through the air, still while holding my hair, till I slammed my back into the wall. I screamed in pain, but he just slammed me against the other wall, then the first one again, back and forth, till I couldn't scream anymore.

I saw the wall approach again, then closed my eyes as I hit it again and again, and when I opened them again, I saw Victor. He was standing behind Samuel. He held out his hands to the sides and lit them on fire, then blasted a ball of fire through the tunnel. After that, there was nothing but a loud whistling sound and darkness. So much darkness.

Chapter 67

HE HAD BLOWN a hole in the sewer. His fire had hit Samuel and burned him. He was lying on his back in the water next to me as I woke up. Victor was standing above me, staring down at me, his hands still a little on fire.

I smiled. "I didn't know you could do that," I said.

He reached down and put out the fire in the water. The explosion had blown a huge hole in the ceiling and soil, and there was air coming in from above us.

Once I got to my feet, we crawled up into the hole. Victor lifted Samuel up through it. Once up on the ground, I realized we had to be on the plantation somewhere. It was dark, but my flashlight still worked. Victor and I carried Samuel back through the plantation, dragging him through the wet snow and back to his house, where Maya and Susan were waiting by the front door.

"Mo-o-o-o-m!"

Maya ran to me, crying. She hugged Victor too, not caring that he didn't like it. She looked down at Samuel, then shed another tear. "I can't believe it. I simply can't."

Finding a key to the crates hanging on the wall, we let

out some poor kid he had kept in there for bloodsucking, and put Samuel in one of his own crates and locked it. Then we let the three other kids out, found an almost life-less boy named Tim, whom Maya knew from school, and freed him, then carried him outside before I called Morten again.

This time he picked up.

"I just got your message," he said. "I'm on my way. What happened? Are you all right? All of you?"

"I'm okay. We all are, I think, more or less shaken, but it's over now. We have more kids drained of blood," I said. "They need help. Could you get ahold of Dr. Williamsen? They need to be taken to the hospital."

"I'll take care of it. And you're sure you're okay?"

I stared at the unconscious Samuel on the floor of the crate. He was still breathing. We had tied him up with the leather straps he had used for his victims, then chained him down with a chain we had found in the basement.

"I will be," I said. "Soon."

"Emma, don't do anything stu…"

I hung up.

My kids came up to me. Skye was with them, already looking better. "What are we going to do about him?" Maya said, looking at her former flame. He was beginning to wither, his skin already peeling off. I guess he never got to drink any of Skye's blood other than the few drops from the cut. Same for Victor's.

"Maybe we should just leave him there," I said with a grin. "Let nature take its course."

Our eyes met. Maya smiled. Victor didn't say anything. He didn't have to. We walked outside and closed the door to the room, then went out to greet Dr. Williamsen and Morten as they arrived and helped them get the poor kids into the ambulance and taken to the ferry that would transport them to the mainland.

Once they left, Morten hugged and kissed me, then asked.

"And Samuel? What happened to him?"

I shrugged, then exchanged a glance with Maya. "He's gone."

"What do you mean, gone?"

"He disappeared," I said.

"Okay. I'll put out a search for him. I'm having this house sealed off until the forensics department can come and take care of it. It might take a few days since there was a big shooting north of Copenhagen today. Something gang-related, but they said they were kind of backlogged when I spoke to them on my way here."

I grabbed him by the shoulder. "There's no rush. And you don't have to put out a search. Samuel won't be coming back."

We walked to my car, Maya's hand in mine. Victor and Skye were already inside it.

"How do you know?" Morten asked, approaching his police car.

"I just do."

"Emma? What aren't you telling me?"

I chuckled.

"Where do you want me to begin?"

Part VI
TWO MONTHS LATER

Chapter 68

SOME LATER SAID they could hear screams coming from the mansion in the nights after we left, screams of the vampire as he suffered a slow death, not being able to get any blood.

In the police report, I read that once the forensic department finally arrived four days later, they found an empty crate inside one of the rooms with a big pile of dust in the bottom of it. When they opened the door, the dust flew out and was scattered in the air. Rumors later said that it sounded like it was whistling *Waltzing Matilda* as it flew away, but those were just rumors and old tales.

Meanwhile, I returned to my writing and soon a book sprang from it. The Dragstedts had been cleared, but their secret was revealed, and they had since kept very low key. Susan got better and went to live with an uncle in the mainland. The kids were back in school, while Skye hung out at my house, Morten still desperately looking for anyone related to her. I kept telling him he wouldn't find anyone, but he insisted it was the right thing to do. I let him, as long as he promised he wouldn't take her away from me unless he found her real home.

Sophia came over on the day I finished the book and had a cup of coffee as usual. She knew the entire story and I had asked her to read along. She was reading the last few pages while nodding and slurping her coffee.

Then she looked up. "It's good. Creepy as hell, but it's really good."

"You think people are going to like a story about a whistling vampire from another world?"

She shrugged. "Sure."

I sighed and grabbed one of the cookies that Sophia had brought. "I'm just nervous that they'll think I'm crazy for writing this. I can hardly tell them it is a true story. No one will believe it."

"Who cares? It's a great story."

I nodded and chewed. Sophia was right. This was my story and it didn't really matter if people liked it or not. I just knew I had to get it out. I had to write it down.

"So, what are you going to call it?"

"I was thinking about *Gone, Vampire, Gone.*"

"Cool. Or—uh—what about *The Girl Who Fell in Love with a Vampire?*" Sophia said.

I nodded, mostly to be polite. "Good too, but a little long. Besides, I'm not sure Maya would ever forgive me if I called it that."

Sophia sniffled. "True. How's she doing by the way?"

"She's okay. Mostly focusing on her graduation. Trying to forget, I think. She doesn't really like to talk about it, so I, of course, I talk about it constantly."

"And Victor?"

"He's back at Fishy Pines where he gets private lessons from HP. I think he's doing pretty well. At least that's what they tell me. He doesn't tell me anything. He only speaks to Skye when he comes home. He only has eyes for her."

Sophia nodded.

"And the blood part? Are you getting over that?"

"I don't know if I can get over it," I said. "I can't stop thinking about it. Why does he have that blood? What does it mean?"

I stared pensively at Sophia, thinking about what Samuel had said in the sewers.

I don't think he is your son.

What the heck was that supposed to mean?

Sophia shrugged. "Guess that's yet another mystery for you to solve, huh? Maybe even another book to write. You could call it *The Mystery of the Green Blood.*"

I laughed and finished my cookie.

"Or maybe you could call it something else," she added.

I nodded with a smile.

"Maybe."

THE END

Afterword

Dear Reader,

Thank you for purchasing *Waltzing Matilda (Emma Frost#11)*. This is the beginning of a new season for Emma and her family. This book is just the beginning of the story. There is so much we still need to know, and I know I left you with many unanswered questions. Like who experimented on them and changed their blood? What happened to John Andersen, the plumber? How and why did Skye and Samuel end up here in our world? Are there more like them? Those and many more questions will be answered later in this series, as we will also learn more about Victor. I'm very excited to continue this story and hope you'll keep reading.

Take care,

Willow

To be the first to hear about new releases and bargains—from Willow Rose—sign up below to be on the VIP List. (I promise not to share your email with anyone else, and I won't clutter your inbox.)

- SIGN UP TO BE ON THE **VIP LIST** HERE :
http://bit.ly/VIP-subscribe

Tired of too many emails? Text the word: "willowrose" to 31996 to sign up to Willow's VIP text List to get a text alert with news about New Releases, Giveaways, Bargains and Free books from Willow.

FOLLOW WILLOW ROSE ON BOOKBUB:
https://www.bookbub.com/authors/willow-rose

Connect with Willow online:

- https://www.facebook.com/willowredrose
- www.willow-rose.net
- http://www.goodreads.com/author/show/4804769.Willow_Rose
- https://twitter.com/madamwillowrose
- madamewillowrose@gmail.com

About the Author

The Queen of Scream aka Willow Rose is a #1 Amazon Best-selling Author and an Amazon ALL-star Author of more than 80 novels. She writes Mystery, Paranormal, Romance, Suspense, Horror, Supernatural thrillers, and Fantasy.

Willow's books are fast-paced, nail-biting page-turners with twists you won't see coming.

Several of her books have reached the Kindle top 20 of ALL books in the US, UK, and Canada.

She has sold more than six million books all over the world.

Willow lives on Florida's Space Coast with her husband and two daughters. When she is not writing or reading, you will find her surfing and watch the dolphins play in the waves of the Atlantic Ocean.

facebook.com/willowredrose

twitter.com/madamwillowrose

instagram.com/madamewillowrose

Books by the Author

HARRY HUNTER MYSTERY SERIES

- ALL THE GOOD GIRLS
- RUN GIRL RUN
- NO OTHER WAY
- NEVER WALK ALONE

MARY MILLS MYSTERY SERIES

- WHAT HURTS THE MOST
- YOU CAN RUN
- YOU CAN'T HIDE
- CAREFUL LITTLE EYES

EVA RAE THOMAS MYSTERY SERIES

- DON'T LIE TO ME
- WHAT YOU DID
- NEVER EVER
- SAY YOU LOVE ME
- LET ME GO
- IT'S NOT OVER

EMMA FROST SERIES

- ITSY BITSY SPIDER
- MISS DOLLY HAD A DOLLY
- RUN, RUN AS FAST AS YOU CAN
- CROSS YOUR HEART AND HOPE TO DIE
- PEEK-A-BOO I SEE YOU

- Tweedledum and Tweedledee
- Easy as One, Two, Three
- There's No Place like Home
- Slenderman
- Where the Wild Roses Grow
- Waltzing Mathilda
- Drip Drop Dead
- Black Frost

JACK RYDER SERIES

- Hit the Road Jack
- Slip out the Back Jack
- The House that Jack Built
- Black Jack
- Girl Next Door
- Her Final Word
- Don't Tell

REBEKKA FRANCK SERIES

- One, Two...He is Coming for You
- Three, Four...Better Lock Your Door
- Five, Six...Grab your Crucifix
- Seven, Eight...Gonna Stay up Late
- Nine, Ten...Never Sleep Again
- Eleven, Twelve...Dig and Delve
- Thirteen, Fourteen...Little Boy Unseen
- Better Not Cry
- Ten Little Girls
- It Ends Here

MYSTERY/THRILLER/HORROR NOVELS

- In One Fell Swoop
- Umbrella Man
- Blackbird Fly
- To Hell in a Handbasket
- Edwina

HORROR SHORT-STORIES

- Mommy Dearest
- The Bird
- Better watch out
- Eenie, Meenie
- Rock-a-Bye Baby
- Nibble, Nibble, Crunch
- Humpty Dumpty
- Chain Letter

PARANORMAL SUSPENSE/ROMANCE NOVELS

- In Cold Blood
- The Surge
- Girl Divided

THE VAMPIRES OF SHADOW HILLS SERIES

- Flesh and Blood
- Blood and Fire
- Fire and Beauty

- BEAUTY AND BEASTS
- BEASTS AND MAGIC
- MAGIC AND WITCHCRAFT
- WITCHCRAFT AND WAR
- WAR AND ORDER
- ORDER AND CHAOS
- CHAOS AND COURAGE

THE AFTERLIFE SERIES

- BEYOND
- SERENITY
- ENDURANCE
- COURAGEOUS

THE WOLFBOY CHRONICLES

- A GYPSY SONG
- I AM WOLF

DAUGHTERS OF THE JAGUAR

- SAVAGE
- BROKEN

Printed in Great Britain
by Amazon